Death of a Doctor
& Other Stories

Death of a Doctor
& Other Stories

by
Elspeth Davie

SINCLAIR-STEVENSON

(.

First published in Great Britain by
Sinclair-Stevenson Limited
7/8 Kendrick Mews
London sw7 3hg, England

Copyright © **1992** by Elspeth Davie

The publisher acknowledges subsidy from the Scottish Arts Council
towards the publication of this volume

British Library Cataloguing in Publication Data
A CIP catalogue record for this book is available from the British Library

ISBN 1-85619-134-6

Photoset by Rowland Phototypesetting Limited
Bury St Edmunds, Suffolk
Printed and bound in Great Britain by
Butler and Tanner Limited, Frome and London

To
Michael Knowles

Acknowledgements

Some of the stories in this collection have been published previously, as follows: *The Man Who Wanted to Smell Books* appeared in the *Literary Review*; *Death of a Doctor* appeared in *New Writing, Scotland (number 7)*; *On Christmas Afternoon* appeared in the *Observer*; *The Morning Mare* appeared in *Chapman Magazine*; *Write on Me* appeared in the *New Edinburgh Review*.

Contents

Death of a Doctor

The doctor's nursing assistant comes into the waiting room rather earlier than usual – just before seven o'clock, in order to say a few words to each person sitting there. The room is already half full. It is midwinter, and throats and chest complaints can be expected. Even though the place is warm enough some people are still wearing scarves. The children have on their knitted woollen caps.

The girl standing in the doorway is an extremely pretty person. In spite of her stiff, white cap and the well-laundered blue overall there is nothing starchy about her. She hesitates for a moment on the threshold, looking about her, then begins to go round the room, saying something quietly to each patient. The words, in fact, are so quiet they can scarcely be heard except by the one person she is speaking to. What she says is: 'I am very, very sorry. I have to tell you that Dr Sneddon died last night.' Often she gives a little touch to a shoulder or to a hand as she says this, and occasionally a light tap on a head as if to instil some unbelieveable message into the hard skull as gently but firmly as possible.

Snow is beginning to fall, though the flakes are still so few they can hardly be seen except when they fly suddenly sideways and glitter close to the waiting-room window. Sometimes they are blown backwards and up towards the high wall of the houses opposite. This long, black building has lighted windows in it and now and then a dark figure can be seen – a woman at a sink, an old man pulling a sweater over his head, a dim room behind, sometimes a set table, and always from the corner the flickering blue light of the TV.

'Dead?' says an elderly man to the assistant. 'Oh, but I've been here a long, long time, and I've come a very long way too. I had to leave my work early. And that wasn't easy, I can tell you.'

This waiting room is by no means a gloomy place. It could almost be called gay with its brightly coloured posters stuck on every inch of the wall – posters about accidents in the home, about diet, about drink and driving and about exercise – showing swimmers, runners, walkers and people bending and stretching in airy bedrooms. There are posters asking for kidney donors, eye donors and blood donors. There are new posters about AIDS and well-known ones calculated to reduce the fear of cancer. There are posters to encourage cervical check-ups and discourage smoking. There are posters on contraceptives and healthy motherhood, on pre-natal clinics and post-natal clinics, on childcare, on vaccination and immunisation. Some of these posters make a dramatic pictorial impact with their flaming frying pans and dizzy drivers steering toward the crash, with their enormously fat and attractively slim people, their mothers with perfect babies and mothers with sad babies. The frenzied businessmen with bulging eyeballs, heading for the heart attack, are hung beside careless people cutting themselves with sharp instruments, or poisoning themselves with badly labelled bottles. Yet whatever these poster-people are doing they are still managing to hang on to life, if only by their fingernails. The elderly man scans them all carefully and seems to feel the lack of something. 'Well, I've been here since six,' he says again, as if this fact in itself should awaken the dead. He stares fixedly at the door as though awaiting a resurrection.

'Yes, I know,' says the girl patiently. She had heard often enough what people can utter under shock. 'And another doctor will be coming tomorrow,' she adds. Yet the man doesn't look shocked, simply tired – tired to death, you could say.

'Well, *when* is the other coming?' he calls after her as she moves on to speak to four people – a young woman in a red coat with her child, and her father and mother, the child's grandparents, on either side of her.

'How can that be?' says the young woman almost brightly when she hears. 'I saw him two days ago. He looked flourishing. Said he'd been golfing. The best round he'd ever had, he told me.'

'You've got to expect anything,' says her father. 'I, for one, am *ready* for anything. That's how I've always gone through life.'

'Well, that's absolute nonsense,' says his wife. 'You're not ready for anything – never have been as long as I've known you. You were never ready when the builders came, never ready for the plumber, always late with the TV licence. When were you ever ready for visitors, even your own grandchildren? How can you be ready for death?'

'It's all beyond her, poor thing,' says the old man, appealing to the nurse with a friendly smile. 'She's speaking of death as a person, isn't she? She's not into the big ideas yet, you see, not into abstractions.'

But the young nursing assistant goes on quickly to take her message round the room. Two pregnant women sitting together take it very badly indeed. Both weep when they hear it, knowing very well how birth and death can be spoken about in the same breath. For a moment the nurse sits between them and puts an arm around their shoulders, praises their hair, their eyes, their complexion, speaks of the happiness of new life, compares their choice of babies' names, asks after their other children and reassures them about the other doctor who will be coming in tomorrow. 'But is he as good, as kind?' they ask anxiously, their hands laid protectively on their bellies as though around precious, easily damaged jars.

There is now a feeling in the room, even amongst those who haven't heard, that something has gone wrong with this place tonight. Several people get up and slowly approach the table where daily and weekly papers are laid out along with certain magazines – romance, beauty, housekeeping for women, with gardening, fishing, engineering and do-it-yourself for men. People are taking a long time to choose. There is a great deal of fussing, rustling and whispering round the table. The women leaf impatiently through those pages devoted to polishes and perfumes for the face and body, polishes and perfumes for the house. Some of the magazines are fearfully old and limp, rough-skinned and dingy. Yet some glamour still remains. Unlike the recent dailies, no tragedy has touched them. Both men and women pick up these newspapers very cautiously tonight, glancing back and forth from the pages to the white-flecked blackness beyond the window as if forcing themselves to relate the innocent white-on-black outside to the sombre, headlined black-on-white within.

The young assistant leaves the pregnant women and continues on her round. Those who suspect nothing out of the ordinary gratefully watch her coming. She is indeed young and pretty, unlike a harbinger of death. On the other hand it seems just possible that she is coming to tell them some comforting news she has picked up about their ailment. Unlikely but possible. In this building all possible and impossible things have been heard and spoken. 'Well, when *is* the other coming?' shouts the elderly man from the other end of the room. In the silence following a man holding a fishing magazine is heard to remark that fishing has saved him.

'Not drugs,' he says, 'not doctors, not diet, not exercise.'

'What was wrong with you then?' says the man beside him. 'What was wrong, that only fishing helped?'

'Nothing wrong with the body,' says the other. 'Not unless you can talk of a body as strung with nerves as a hung-up puppet. Nerves were what was wrong. Nerves and nothing else.'

'Sounds bad,' says the one beside him. 'I've never had that. But what have fish got to do with it?'

'Casting a rod over a deep pool is what it is. Flicking the fly over a flowing stream. Not a sound from the bushes on a still day and not a ripple on the pool. The one and only thing that's cured a bad bout of nerves. No, don't talk to me about the medicine men, don't give me the psychiatrists. This is Nature, you understand. Or maybe you don't. Not many do these days.'

'But there's the tooth-and-claw bit, of course,' says the one beside him. 'How do you square that?'

'I don't. I've seen creatures gobbling one another up while I sat peacefully on the bank, insects biting, tangling to the death with other insects, great bugs chewing up small bugs. I've seen cats purring and pawing over mice, grown men forcing poison down rabbit holes. Screams and agony all around on a summer's day.'

'Funny that doesn't get on your nerves,' says the other.

'Well. I count myself one of these animals, of course.

7

Maybe that's the reason. I've got used to my own cruel breed, for better or worse. I'm pretty tough, I daresay. Though I admit I came round here this evening because I didn't feel so good.'

Having got through papers and magazines there is little for the patients to do except watch the girl making the round of the room. Everyone stares at her – the women even more than the men. Their feelings are mixed. Some who have been flicking through romantic stories ask themselves whether the doctor has ever been in love with her. They wonder what the lonely, ageing wives make of such girls – the beautiful attendants of doctors and dentists, the glamorous private secretaries of business executives and politicians, the gorgeous guardian angels of every clergyman, spiritual director and bishop, the comely companions of all-night petrol-pump attendants, the stunning policewomen and the teacher's pretty helpmate. Tonight the thought of this weakens their resistance more than the flu or the sore throat, more even than the asthma. The awful injustice of it all grabs them in the pit of the stomach like the start of labour pains. True enough, somebody said, the wife is everything at the end of the day. A faithful wife is more precious than rubies. Rubies, was it, or was it emeralds? Emeralds or diamonds or just plain pearls? It is always terribly hard to get these jewel qualities of wives properly sorted out.

'And when is the *other* coming?' shouts the old man again from the end of the room.

'Just hold your tongue, you, and show some respect!' a woman exclaims.

Some of the children are getting bored now. There are a few toys near the table but they are for the younger ones. The older group ignore the scarlet wagon on wheels, the drum, the yellow truck carrying bricks, the

moth-eaten teddy bear. The tired babies, their eyelids a
faint blue with sleepiness, have started to wail and are
being bounced on their mothers' knees. The girl in the
blue overall watches the older children for a while, then
holding a small boy and girl by the hand she takes them
to the window and lets them kneel, each on a chair, to
watch the flakes blowing outside. Now more people can
be seen peering from kitchens across the street. Some
there have almost forgotten they are looking into a waiting room. They have stayed so long staring out from
darkening, empty rooms it seems they are envying the
carefree closeness of the crowd opposite – the lively talk,
the table covered with papers and coloured journals, the
toys, the children playing, and in their midst this amiable young woman who is exceedingly attentive, who
bends and speaks intimately to each person in turn like
the good hostess at a party. The food is lacking, certainly, but no doubt there is a laden table somewhere
behind the scenes.

By this time the nursing assistant has reached a very
old man sitting close to the gas fire. He is holding a
small sporting paper and his hand shakes so wildly the
sound of paper is out of all proportion to the size of
page. It resembles some gale-swept poster tearing itself
off the sea wall. His head is shaking too. To those who
watch, it looks as if he is not at all startled by the girl's
message, but rather affirming every word she says with
a violent nodding of the head as if – unlike the others –
he is agreeing silently but energetically that death is
inevitable, not surprising at all and must be continually
accepted without question. The girl braces his shoulders
firmly for a second and passes on to a youngish couple
sitting together by the window. 'Will he be long over
the patients tonight, do you think?' says the woman
glancing over her shoulder. 'We've such a distance to

get home. If this goes on we might even be stuck out there. This time last year the car scarcely got through the last two miles on the hill. Of course, I know he can't help it. But will he be long? My husband's in pain. It actually took him an age to get down into this chair. He can neither sit down nor stand up, you see. And as for lying! Even a few pills for the night would help. Of course the doctor can't help it. He's no say over his time when the surgery's full. That's the worst of practices these days.'

The young assistant is thoughtful for a moment as if considering carefully this question of time. She raises her eyes and looks into a mirror between two posters on the opposite wall – one persuading people to stop smoking, the other discreetly mentioning kidney donation.

'No, they'll never get a kidney out of me,' says the grandfather of the child as he follows the direction of the girl's eyes. 'Not a kidney, not an eye! I'm keeping every bit of myself to the grave, and every drop of blood to the last. It's hard enough keeping myself together as it is, and getting harder every day!'

In the mirror the girl's face looks smooth and youthful. To the old people it seems she could never be thinking of the passing of time, far less about death. Still she conscientiously gives her news to the once snow-bound couple who lean forward attentively to listen, then grab one another's hands. This young husband who is supposed to be unable either to sit down or to stand up, gets to his feet in one straight, sudden movement like a dancer who raises his partner with him by force of an unexpected discord in the musical score. The three of them stand together for a moment – the young couple with the nurse. Slowly she presses them down into their chairs again. She takes great care doing this – putting one hand on the woman's shoulder, supporting the man's back with the other and making sure their feet are firmly set on the floor – planting them, so it seems, like fragile plants into deep earth before she turns away.

Beside them are two men discussing the repair of an old car. The older has his arm encased in plaster from wrist to elbow and he holds it out stiffly in a half-salute towards the middle of the room. Once in a while children come up and tap it curiously with a fingernail. Unlike the drum on the table it makes a dull, heavy sound. These men have already heard what has been said to the couple on their right. The nurse stops beside them only for a moment. 'Well, that's the saddest thing,' says the youngest man, 'and he can't have been much older than me. I always liked that doctor – loved isn't too strong a word. He came once in the middle of the night – when I could hardly breathe, when I was in such a panic I thought it was the finish of me. Believe it or not, I started to breathe again the minute that man came through the door. And when he started to talk to me things were OK as if nothing had happened. What did he talk about? I remember something about his mother's hens. Anyway the sheer stupidity of those hens, clucking and scraping through that night, brought me round. And then the smooth, harmless eggs lying there in the morning straw. Well, the whole thing calmed me. Whenever I have another attack I think of hens. What else he did for me I *can't* remember. The poor young man. To tell you the truth I'm terrified to hear that news. I feel bereft. I'm sorry I sound so heartless – talking about myself,' he says to the nurse.

'Not heartless at all,' she replies, noticing that he is pale and beginning to gasp a little like a man forcing his head suddenly out of a strong wave. She takes his hand and draws a deep breath. When his colour returns and they are both breathing slowly and regularly together, she moves on. Once again from the far corner of the room the old man shouts louder than ever: 'When is the other *coming*?'

It is snowing heavily now, and with their fingers the children follow the crisscrossing tracks down the windowpane or make sudden, swooping movements with their hands as the flakes blow upwards on a gust of wind. In the windows of the houses opposite several people are still staring across. Some have even left the TV screen to watch. The ghostly blue light still flickers behind them as they peer enviously down into this real, lit room full of flesh-and-blood men, women and children with their genuine fire, their real toys, papers and pictures and all presided over by a friendly girl, prettier than a TV star. This girl has made the full circle of the room and now she reaches the door where she stands in silence. Everyone waits for her to speak, even the children loading the yellow truck with the last brick and the kneeling snowflake-tracers who have now climbed down and are rubbing their red knees. The watchers in the windows opposite, seeing nothing but her moving lips, wonder if she is welcoming the company, promising something better to come, or already on the point of saying goodbye. 'I am so sorry I had to give you this news tonight,' says the girl. 'It's a terrible shock for all of us. You've waited here too long, I know. But I thought it better to tell each one of you.' She puts her hand on the door and tells them that another doctor will be here early the next day and that meantime any emergency can be seen around the corner in the next street. She gives a name, a street number, a telephone number. And now she waits for the patients to leave. Slowly they get up, one by one, and come across. Some touch her quickly on the arm, in passing, or on the shoulder, as she has done to them. One or two give the crown of her head a quick, light stroke. These are all cautious touches as if to discover if she is truly flesh, blood and bone, to make sure she will still be there for them tomorrow and the day after and all the weeks to come, if need be. Yet all these discreet touches have done something to the girl. Her hard, shore-substance is being gradually dissolved by this sea of need. The determination is wavering slightly. The last people to leave see that she is in tears.

In spite of the movement through the door the waiting room is not yet empty. An old woman, sitting where she has sat for the last half hour, is still there, knitting. Opposite, on the other side of the table, a serious middle-aged man is still engrossed in his book. Long ago the nurse has spoken to them, but it is as if they had never heard. She approaches the woman. 'The others are going now,' she says. 'I'm afraid you'll have to go off as well. You see, I have to close the place in a few minutes.' For a while the knitting needles click on more rapidly than ever. Then the old woman drops the red, woollen scarf for an instant to remark:

'I am waiting to see my doctor! No, not *any* doctor. My *own* doctor! Even if I have to wait all night!'

'Will you help me?' says the girl, moving across to the reading man. 'She doesn't seem to know what's happened, though I tried to tell her. Perhaps you can help. I'm sure you understand.'

'Yes, I understand all right, but I can't help,' says the man. 'Of course I'd *like* to help. But I can never get this death business into my head straight off. I don't just mean the doctor's death. Any death. It's stupid, isn't it? At my age. Utterly stupid and childish. But do you mind if I sit here for a while longer till I get the hang of it? Then I'll certainly try to persuade the old girl to leave with me. Do you mind?'

'No, I don't mind at all,' says the girl, 'and I'll sit myself for a bit. There's not all that hurry.' The three of them sit silently and apart with only the sound of needles clicking and the surreptitious turning of the pages of a book. After a while the girl goes through a door leading to a cupboard and comes out five minutes later with a tray, a pot of tea, three cups and saucers, sugar, milk, three biscuits on a plate. She pours the tea and hands it round.

Opposite, the lonely TV watchers, peering from dark rooms through flurries of snow, can scarcely believe their eyes. Oh, the luck of some people! This easy get-together, the comfortable tea-talk and the friendly warmth on a freezing night. How they have missed all this, not just this night but every night! Yes, every night of their lives this very thing has managed to go past them without their knowing it.

The man with the book makes the first move. He goes across to the old woman and takes her ball of wool between his hands. 'What's this you're knitting?' he asks.

'A scarf for my third grandchild,' she replies. 'Two years old next month.'

The man presses the soft, scarlet ball against his cheek and stares at her. 'Will you let me take you home in my car?' he says. 'I'm going to take the young lady home too. So you'll be perfectly safe,' he adds.

'Yes, I'll go,' she replies. 'Though I'd always feel perfectly safe here, of course, even if I was the last one left. As a matter of fact I always feel safe when I'm waiting to see the doctor, though I do happen to know there are certain folk who feel they've never been nearer danger or even death when they set foot inside this waiting room. But there's really no need for that, is there?'

'None at all,' says the man. 'Come along now before it gets worse out there.' He takes her one arm, the girl takes the other, and they leave the room.

The snow is driving down so thickly against the windows that, fortunately, no watcher from the opposite side can now see this desolate, vacant room, its empty chairs arranged as in some séance which – deserted by all its members – still hopefully awaits the return of one punctual and devoted spirit.

Absolute Delight

*M*r Roderick Mason knew that, sooner or later, he would be forced to order all his shoes from special catalogues because he had what was politely called in the trade 'difficult feet'. One day he saw in a newspaper the advertisement of a shoe firm which seemed to know of all the infirmities and deformities of the human foot since man had descended from the trees on to hard ground. Mr Mason immediately sent for the catalogue of this firm. It arrived almost by return of post, heavy as a telephone directory and packed with coloured pictures of all sizes and shapes of shoe. He was delighted to see that none of them were for easy feet. They were for feet with awkwardly shaped heels and fallen arches, for feet with bunions and twisted toes, for feet too narrow or too broad, too short or too long. No normal foot graced these pages. But the catalogue reassured and comforted. It promised blissful comfort against every mishap the human foot might suffer upon the cruel earth. Mr Mason had always dreaded entering shoe shops with his difficult feet which were both large and very badly shaped. But one day a kind assistant simply called them 'strange feet' as she knelt with the tenth pair of discarded shoes behind her on the floor. From then on he himself preferred to call them 'strange' rather than difficult. Nevertheless, a different word, however delicate, brought no change to his feelings about his feet. He went on studying the shoe catalogue – absorbing the descriptions, the rules of exchange, the prices and promises with the seriousness and intensity of a scholar.

One, final detail on the last page never failed to catch his eye. It was the phrase: 'Send back if not Absolutely Delighted.' It was this Absolute Delight that intrigued him. Some faint presentiment floated through his mind that this was not unlike a challenge thrown to his difficult feet. A duel perhaps? A fight to the finish? Had he himself ever felt absolutely delighted with anything in the whole fifty-one years of his life? Delight? Yes, of course. But *absolute* delight? This was a huge claim which – being an honest and a cautious man – he couldn't bring himself to take up.

Mr Mason had other difficulties in life besides the problem of his feet. Although he was now a teacher of English in a good school, he had once been an excellent classical scholar. But this subject had long ago been almost entirely pushed aside for really useful subjects, useful in the home and in life – subjects such as woodwork, home economics and practical dressmaking which he regarded as a lot easier but a good deal less important than the divine discord and immortal relationships between gods and goddesses. He regarded the figures of myth, both good and bad, with awe and affection. When called for, they had stepped, elegantly, from shells, trees, clouds and the clefts of rocks. Unwelcomed, they could throw thunderbolts around with grace and skilfully draw daggers of lightning from the clouds. Whether angry or benign, in fact, Mr Mason believed they had an enormous amount to teach the ruffianly world he lived in.

Though the English teacher was liked by his colleagues he had latterly been considered a rather eccentric man who, during the last week or so, had tended to ask rather awkward personal questions. This was unexpected, seeing he'd been thought to have little interest in persons, but only in books. Indeed these questions sounded out of character for such a seemingly discreet and private individual. 'Have you ever felt absolute delight?' he would ask, having buttonholed someone in the corridors or on the stairs. These stairs were scrubbed every day with hard, hygienic soap, yet the smell of sweaty plimsolls hung continually about them from one term's end to the next. They had never been thought of as the place to stop and enquire about happiness. It was tactless, to say the least. Yet Mr Mason would press on. 'Does delight exist?' he would say. 'If so, does absolute delight come, in your opinion, from love, money, sex, friendship, books, music, travel, a good digestion? Or does it,' he would add, as if by happy afterthought, 'by any chance come from well-fitting shoes?' People were apt to give him very different answers – some adding all sorts of high-flown ideas of their own. The history master wished to become the powerful editor of a learned journal while the head of music dreamed only of writing new cadenzas to several well-known concertos. Some, for the sake of a little peace and quiet, simply replied it was indeed true: absolute delight must surely lie in a really comfortable pair of shoes.

At last, from his catalogue, Roderick Mason made his choice. He wrote away for a fine pair of strong, strapped summer shoes from the firm, and received them on the Saturday morning a few days later. He tried them on at once and walked through to the kitchen. True, he was absolutely delighted with them as he stood frying bacon and egg on the stove. He was quite delighted with them as he walked round by the corner to post some letters. As he walked back on a long, circuitous route by way of the grocer's he experienced a painful doubt at the heel. When he reached the shop he decided he had to sit down while the grocer placed the butter, cheese, eggs and a packet of cereal together on the counter. 'Too warm for this time of year, isn't it?' remarked the shopkeeper's wife, glancing at the customer's drawn face. Mr Mason nodded silently with dread at his heart. It was not only the heel now, but the middle toe of both feet. His parcel was packed up and ready to hand over. Mr Mason didn't rise from his chair at once. His face was pale. He asked the grocer quietly if he had ever experienced absolute delight in his life. The young grocer – a modest man of few words – looked embarrassed by the exceedingly personal nature of this question, so unlike the newspaper talk and remarks about the weather usual at this time in the morning. There were a few other persons in the shop now who appeared to be waiting intently for his answer. Above all there was his wife to consider. It seemed to the grocer, who knew how to handle eggs with great lightness and tact, that his customer was rather grossly overstepping the limits of delicacy.

Mr Mason limped home in a state of excruciating pain. When he examined his feet later he had to be honest. His new shoes had not actually drawn blood. They had not permanently damaged his toes as far as he could make out. He placed them in their box and sent them back the next day, politely stating his regret and disappointment at having to return them. He had tried them on and walked a short distance as recommended. But he was not absolutely satisfied, he said. He could not bring himself to write the word 'delighted'. There followed a short interval and then one morning came an identical, well-produced colourful catalogue with its pitiful descriptions of difficult feet, plus an agreeable letter saying how sorry they were that the shoes had not been entirely satisfactory, but that no doubt he would find exactly what he desired in the enclosed catalogue. If he was not absolutely delighted with his next order when it arrived he must not hesitate to send the shoes back, following which any complaint would be given the closest attention by a group of persons who had nothing but his perfect comfort in mind. Mr Mason waited some time before replying. Then he wrote that he had studied the second catalogue with great care. Strangely enough, he had found it was no different from the last one. He had not changed his mind. He was not contemplating buying any other shoes displayed therein.

There was a long silence now – a long, compassionate, concerned silence as it turned out. And then came a letter, more in sorrow than in anger, indicating that there was a large group of very caring, loving people at their end – people who had sat communing together for a very long time trying to figure out, almost prayerfully it seemed, what exactly could be wrong with poor Mr Mason's feet and even with his psychological outlook that he was not able to find even one item that pleased him in their extremely attractive and comprehensive catalogue. They hoped that Mr Mason was able to get out of the house. If not, would he care to have a personal visit from a representative of the firm when he could try on as many shoes as he liked at his leisure? There would, of course, be absolutely no obligation to take any shoes unless he was perfectly satisfied.

Now, indeed, Mr Mason was totally silent as if, as far as the outside world was concerned, any move or sound from him would set up a great rustling and unpacking of shoes from boxes in the distant city. He could imagine the little ladders being set up against the shelves, and the search beginning. No doubt his awkward psyche was being discussed, the peculiarities of his physique being bandied about, his letters read and read again. Finally, his stubborn silence would be commented upon and various views put forward as to how it should be broken. Perhaps already they were choosing ambassadors who would come to root him out and thrust shoes upon his feet.

But now as days and weeks passed Mr Mason gradually became happy and hopeful that the thing had ended at last. He wore his old shoes continually. Certainly they were far from comfortable but now he wondered why he had ever bothered about finding new ones. When, after a fair interval, another catalogue arrived, the postman found it impossible to force it through the slit in his door. This was because a new leaflet had been inserted into the centre of its pages – more colourful, more explicit than the other, describing all the pains of human feet, their tender toes, bent bones and badly matching heels, feet that, in fact, seemed no earthly good for standing on, let alone walking. When he had finished studying this latest catalogue, Mr Mason began to marvel at a deity able to introduce anything as complex as the human foot into man's evolution. Compared with the foot, it seemed that the brain was a comparatively simple and efficient affair. Several times now during his wakeful nights he woke in despair and sat on the edge of his bed, staring at his feet. They had served him up till now without too much trouble. But if the worst came to the worst he could teach in his bedroom slippers, shop in his sand-shoes and do his housework in his climbing socks. It was only when he thought of further catalogues thumping through his letterbox that his heart failed him.

But now, out of the night, the winged messenger of

those ancient gods whom he revered, was flying down to prompt him. In the morning he wrote what he believed to be his final note to the shoe firm. It was very polite and clear: 'I thank you for all your help and concern about my feet. Yes indeed, I have difficulty in finding the right kind of shoe, though I admit I have certain peculiarities that are not listed in your excellent catalogue. I'm afraid the main trouble is that I happen to need wings on all my shoes. In fact I can say, without undue boasting, that I resemble Hermes, the divine messenger of the gods. I am, of course, proud of these wings. But naturally, I am not always in the air and would therefore be grateful for a pair of shoes which would fit my rather special requirements – or, in other words, shoes in which I could both walk and fly. I await my order confidently, bearing in mind that if I am not absolutely delighted I may return the shoes intact.'

Mr Mason waited for two or three weeks. After the third week he walked out on Sunday to the corner shop in a pair of blue bedroom slippers embroidered with yellow parrots – a present from his niece – and was congratulated for having such sensible feet amongst the tight shoes and high heels of other shoppers. In the fourth week he bought his milk and rolls clad in a black and scarlet dressing-gown and was praised for being an utterly free and happy spirit. Though this seemed to him to be wildly over the mark, there was nevertheless some truth in it. Mr Mason ordered nothing and received nothing for the rest of his life. He ignored the promises of house-cleaning equipment, luxury cars and free holidays. He let slip the offer of an exercise bicycle and a Chinese dinner service, and allowed the chance of packets of ten-pound notes to waft past him as though on the morning breeze. One day the offers stopped abruptly. His sacks were still enormously heavy as he carted them downstairs to the street. He took a thought for the hearts of all rubbish collectors. But his own was as light as a bird.

On Christmas Afternoon

9 A young boy, in the midst of a great Christmas Day party, suddenly came bursting out of one of the upper rooms of the house and began to descend a long flight of stairs. The screams of the children, snapping off as the door shut behind him, seemed to propel him down the first few steps and almost sent him headlong down the rest, for his hands were pressed hard over his ears and his eyes were screwed tight shut. His panic had been sudden and overwhelming. For a moment the whole house, vibrating and jangling with light and noise, had become for him unstable, like a huge stone slipping out of place into some dangerous position. Now, in the comparative silence of the staircase he waited for it to right itself, steadying his hand on the banisters and looking out of the long hall window into the garden, where the trees stood absolutely still and black against the green afternoon sky. All the intense silence and coldness into which, in imagination, he could escape, lay beyond that window, and at the sight of that static world, breathing deeply its freezing air, he gradually grew calmer again. Cautiously now he began to make his way down towards the room below, treading softly and glancing round to see that his flight from one world into another had not been noticed. But there was no-one about, no movement except the lamps

29

swaying a little as the thumping of feet began again from overhead.

Three parties were going on in that house. In the top room the children's party was in full swing; below that on the first floor the grown-ups had started to dance; and on the ground floor beside the dining room elderly people had gathered together for safety against the excitement of the rest of the house. But this boy had missed the labels and the introductions; he had come in at the end of supper and afterwards had found himself swept up with the children to the highest room. Very soon he discovered that this, after all, was not the place where he should be. Reddening with shame, he discovered the length of his arms and his legs compared with the others. He could reach up and bring down balloons which had lodged on the highest ledges, or pull out the streamers twisted about the centre light. The little grace which he had got made him conspicuous in the dancing games where the other children could only hop, and his own silence, amid bursts of screaming, frightened him and made his heart beat violently as though he had indeed jumped and screamed harder than all the rest. Now, standing in the middle of the staircase, he brushed off the silvery dust which had fallen on his shoulder and sleeve from frosted decorations, trying in that gesture to brush off every trace of childishness before entering the room below. But when he got to the door he leaned a long time against it with his head upon his folded arms, feeling the drum pounding through his temples, hearing the dancers passing close to him with a sound like a mysterious breeze blowing close to the ground. Even outside the door he felt the moving air on his legs, and when he opened it the hair was lifted from his scalp by a hot wind – a sensation like that which he had experienced only in moments of intense joy or fear.

Dozens of couples were sliding quickly past down the length of the room – a long, narrow room like a hall, not glinting and sparkling with tinsel and shining balls like the place he had just left, but glowing in red light, with deep avenues of shadow down both sides. Great lights swathed in red paper hung from the ceiling, swaying with the vibration of the room, and enormous red and green paper balls dangled against the heads of the tallest dancers, who knocked them sideways with their fists, shouting and laughing. The boy began to walk carefully along one side where chairs were lined up, half in shadow. Stiff girls sat waiting here, staring in front of them and fingering, as though they were charms, those brooches and bracelets which they had unwrapped that morning and put on for the first time that afternoon. Now and then some fierce movement from the centre knocked the boy sideways against their legs and he saw their eyes stare up at him, reproachful but indifferent, because he was not yet a man, and not yet to be reckoned with. He longed to sit there with them, because he knew that they were out of the dance for ever and therefore safe; but as though aware of this thought they became quickly hostile. Even their view of the dance was blocked now, as they leaned this way and that behind him, craning their necks and raising sharp elbows like a crowd of flurried birds. He went quickly on.

Right at the end of the room in the opposite corner there was another door leading down to the dining room, and towards this he slowly made his way. Long green fronds of streamer caught his shoulder, the hems of swirling silk frocks brushed against his legs, and gusts of air, smelling of powder and dust and singeing crêpe paper, made his head swim as he wound in and out of light and shadow along the slippery floor. Sometimes he got caught within the circle of the dance and couples slid about him, laughing and pressing him off with their elbows; and once with a great effort he broke through and stumbled off as far into shadow as he could, right in behind the row of chairs under the pillars of the room. But even here there were people. Men and women sat in pairs together on the floor against the wall, their heads turned towards one another, their legs stretched limply out in front of them. Even before he could see them clearly he was stepping clumsily across these legs, while their heads turned and they waited silently for him to go. His clumsy recoil from this territory of love-making made them aware it was a child who had intruded, and an odd one at that – a child who plainly showed in his face a disbelief in the happiness either of their world or his own. For a moment all whispering and kissing stopped as he went by, and they drew in their legs to let him pass. But the boy had only one thought now, to reach the door opposite by plunging blindly through the midst of the dancers underneath the orchestra at the top of the room. Over his head the saxophone and the drum were working up to a frenzied crescendo; the noise for a moment was so great it seemed to shatter the whole room, and then suddenly it ceased and through the strong drift of dancers returning to their seats he moved on with his head down. Occasionally somebody would stand in his way to take a look at him, and catching a glimpse of his face a woman asked:

'Is anything wrong?'

'Can't you see? He's trying to get back for a second helping,' replied her partner. They made way for him now, laughing good-naturedly and pushing him on, and he was able to make a flying leap for the door through the clear space in front of him. As though from a long distance he heard their laughter as it closed behind him.

The room which he now entered was a place set apart from everything that was going on in the rest of the house, cosy and secluded as a plush-lined box. It seemed to the elderly people who sat there that he had not seen them at all, even though to get through the room he had to wind his way through their armchairs. He moved like somebody in a dream, bumping against them, shifting cushions from under their elbows and catching the ends of knitting needles with his awkward movements; even the gossip was disturbed by his distracted muttering as he passed by. They leaned forward curiously to look at him as he approached the mirror above the fireplace, chafing their hands and pulling their wraps closer for a few minutes as he stood blocking out the heat. He was beside himself now, looking at the boy in the glass as he would at a stranger, shocked by the whiteness of the face, the anxious lips and black stricken eyes peering close to him, the dark hair all on end. Vaguely he saw the heads behind him, leaning together, but he did not look round. On his left, above a short flight of steps, was the last door he would need to pass through in that house; he knew that from the room below, free for the first time that day, he could make his escape.

But the room was not empty as he had imagined. Mr Barns, who stood at the other end of the dining room beside the fire, could not see the boy's face clearly, but he imagined from his appearance that he must have frightened him. They faced one another down the length of a huge table, a magnificent wreck of a table, strewn with tangled heaps of decoration paper, cracker wrappings and burst balloons; ragged chrysanthemums hung askew from their vases, and against the white tablecloth big red and yellow jellies which had not been touched shimmered in glass dishes, and mounds of pink blancmange toppled and slit apart with every thump of the drum from the room above. All down the table there was a faint rattling of glasses and spoons and Mr Barns did not attempt to make himself heard until the music stopped. He was wearing a large Father Christmas robe, dusty and badly ripped up one side; and with one foot on a chair, twisted uncomfortably round, he was attempting to sew up this tear. When he looked up again the boy had moved down the room, and as he came into the light Mr Barns was aware that approaching him now was a strange being, a haunted, unnatural child who should have been shouting with joy like the rest of them, but because of some earthquake in the centre of his private world had landed just on the outside of normal experience. He was a child who wished to be hidden at once, captured or embraced – whatever would take him out of sight quickly and put him into darkness. Mr Barns had never seen quite this expression on a face before, and it occurred to him now as he saw it that this, then, was the real meaning of a displaced person.

Mr Barns felt extraordinarily shy for the first time in his life. More than ever now he felt that it had been particularly foolish of his hostess to choose him to play the part of the children's saint. He knew that he was not specially good with children, he had none of his own, and moreover he had always hoped to keep out of the way of the so-called difficult ones who had to be handled in a special way, known only to psychologists. The boy was beside him now, staring so hard with his black eyes that Mr Barns felt that perhaps he must appear in some way a ludicrous figure, recognised even by the boy as being thoroughly unsuited to the part.

'At the very last minute I find this enormous tear,' he explained rather severely. 'No doubt the last Santa Claus

34

was afraid to tell our hostess. Moreover, when I come to put on the mask I find that half the beard has been torn away, and that means half my afternoon is to be spent searching the whole house for glue and cotton wool as well as the needle and thread. Luckily the cotton wool was easy; there was too much snow on top of the Christmas tree and I soon removed that.' He sat down and began to stitch again. As he had suspected, the boy said nothing, but sat down on a chair beside him. Gradually Mr Barns decided that he would simply forget about the child, that he would not even try to understand him, but let him sit by his side, half covered by the red cloak, until he had come round again. They sat in silence, listening to the music stopping and starting again, and now and then hearing faint thumps and screams from the top of the house. Sometimes the man glanced down at the boy and they would exchange a smile which was a little ironic, because they were both out of it all, and both, for different reasons which neither of them could put into words, glad to be out of it.

'Now for the great moment,' said Mr Barns suddenly, getting up and consulting his watch. It seemed that this was a moment which the whole house had also anticipated. The music had stopped some time ago, and now there was a tremendous shuffling of feet from above and a grating of chairs pushed back. 'Now they are bringing in the tree,' said Mr Barns, nervously buttoning up his gown. 'In a minute the children will come down.' He was putting on the mask and hood now, exchanging the tired and anxious face of middle age for that of a rosy, benevolent old man. The child was standing up now, looking at him as though at one stroke he had lost everything in his world. It was a desperate look, out of all proportion to anything which had gone before, and having in it the very essence of

every change and loss in love. It made his sharp, small
face look suddenly old and rather ugly. Now from the
top of the house they could hear the door opening and
a great rush of feet down the stairs, then sudden shouts
of triumph as the tree came in view.

'I'm going up now,' said Mr Barns, going over to the
great sack in the corner, 'but I'll need some help handing
these out, and besides there's all the stuff on the tree as
well. You'd be a good hand at that, I think. Are you
coming up?' His question was casual, but he had
removed his mask to ask it, and now he waited for the
reply as he might await some decision of tremendous
moment. Many expressions which he could not understand passed across the boy's face, as though he looked
back not only through the hours which had just been,
but through years, further back than any normal child
had a right to remember. But when he met Mr Barns'
eyes again he had returned to that present moment and
place.

'Yes,' he replied, keeping his eyes fixed on the other,
'I'm coming up with you.'

Everybody had come from all parts of the house now
to the dancing-room above. The room where the old
people had sat was quite empty, and as they went
through it they could hear the tremendous hum of
excitement beyond them through the closed door. Mr
Barns now opened this door, quietly pushing himself
through; but at once there was a roof-raising yell of
triumph, a tremendous prolonged roar of welcome. Mr
Barns retreated for a moment, peering back a little anxiously through his eye-slits at the boy behind.

'All this is coming to you one day when you're grown
up,' he said. 'You'll get this sort of welcome somewhere, mark my words, and without dressing up for it
either.' He told himself, for the sake of his conscience,

that though this had never been true for him or for any other person in his experience, it might possibly be true for this boy, whose eyes, in spite of his fear, shone with such astounding and terrifying hope. Together they went into the cheering room.

Write on Me

A small boy and his father were going around a large exhibition of paintings in a crowded gallery. The man knew something about pictures. He had even tried his hand at painting when he was young and was disappointed that it had come to nothing. Yet this was mixed with relief. His own parents had known artists of all kinds and had conveyed to him, as a young man, that all attempts at perfection in any art were doomed. Even those who recognised excellence in the past were bound, they maintained, to be continually depressed by finding it totally missing in themselves. Now, warily, from a distance, he watched his own son staring at a painting, and wondered exactly what he was seeing.

What the small boy was seeing at that moment was a large square of canvas covered with a smooth, thick coating of pure white paint. There was no colour on it and no mark of any kind. Occasionally one or two people from the crowd would pause there for a moment – not only to laugh or point – but also, as it were, to rest. The expanse of white paint was curiously seductive. Enclosed by its broad frame, it gave, to some, a sense of total peace and safety. Not everyone felt safe, however. Some felt that if they stood too long staring, they might lose their voice, miss the meaning of the thing – if it had meaning – and, at worst, fall through pure whiteness into space and lose their identity for ever. The boy's father also felt this as he stared silently at the square, momentarily petrified, as if vainly searching for himself. Indeed he would have much preferred if it had been a large mirror instead of a canvas – simply for the safety of his own company as well as the reflection of all those others who were walking by. Once he signed to a solemn-looking man who was standing near.

'Take a look at this,' he said quietly, trying to make his voice sound merely casual and amused.

'Certainly not! I *have* already looked at it and there is nothing there!' the man irritably replied and went rapidly on his way. Most people were going quickly past down the long gallery. Having now no company and no recognisable shapes to hold onto in the picture, the man kept his eyes firmly fixed on his son. The white painting was not set very high on the wall, but even so the little boy came up only a few inches above the bottom corner of the frame. He seemed suddenly impatient of his father's fixed, insistent stare and, sensing this, the man moved away down the room and set himself to studying busier, friendlier canvases.

But his small son had come unexpectedly on something that fascinated him in one corner of the white canvas. He saw some wiry letters and crouched down to study them. It was not a name, not a title, not even an initial as might have been thought at first glance. Three words were here, written delicately but clearly in fine, black ink: *Write on Me*. The little boy had not long learned to read and write well. He was still rather sensitive about words and white spaces – how they looked and what they meant. Yet he felt at once that the words in the corner were a faint but direct plea to himself. He looked quickly round to see if anyone was near. Then he took from his pocket a birthday present from his mother: his first fountain pen – a fine-nibbed one, filled that morning with strong, blue ink. He then crouched down to the picture and below the words in the corner wrote in fine script – fine but not cautious: 'I love this.'

A few people were casually approaching that side of the room. Two women detached themselves from the rest and one bent down to the picture.

'Do you see this?' she said to her friend. 'Somebody's answered it, anyway. Obviously a child. But I wouldn't mind following it up myself. *Write on Me*. What a chance! Think what Shakespeare would have made of that. But all I can think of is this list I've got in my bag reminding me to get a small brown loaf and two pork pies. Not much of the immortal line about that, is there?'

'The bread wouldn't look out of place,' said her friend, 'but I'd leave out the pork pies, if I were you. Somehow, they've never been thought to have much spirit about them.'

But her companion, a teacher, had changed her mind. She bent down and with the red pen she used for corrections she wrote: 'Thank you, but I don't know what to say.'

Suddenly they were aware of hurried, booted steps coming towards them. The man had an official blue and red band on his arm. His face was scarlet.

'WHAT IN ALL HELL IS GOING ON?' he shouted.

'We were simply answering a command to write something,' said the older woman. 'My words were feeble. Your own just now were magnificent, though I know you can't put them down here. Naturally your job is to protect canvases, not deface them. But this was a plea, and I've never had to answer a passionate plea before. Yes, I *did* use a red pen. It's supposed to remove inhibitions if you don't know the person well. It didn't work for me, and my friend here is too timid to write a word, far less a line. Are you a letter-writer yourself?' she asked the official.

'Don't you worry,' he said, 'I'll be writing to the Governors of this gallery as soon as I leave the place. And there'll be the devil to pay, to put it mildly.' He marched off in the direction of the door.

More and more people were now gathering to look at the white canvas and to read the message in its corner. Few went off without writing something and most of it was written not only in ordinary lead pencil but in rainbow-hued pens, in smudgy, coloured crayon and even bits of black charcoal. Soon it seemed that raw feeling had miraculously flowered into every colour of the spectrum, but as the afternoon went on the light in the room also began to change. The canvas was now both cool and warm. A cold blue light was falling from the roof window, mixed with the still rosy light from the long west windows where the sun was gradually going down. Now more people, having heard of some incident in the main room, were entering the place before it shut. Soon they were encouraged by what they saw in the white canvas to be more daring in their own marks and words. The joy and grief that had been set down in abrupt words and phrases was expressed by these latecomers in longer lines of script and even in actual verse. Many had added their initials.

A teacher of music and his friend in business came up close and studied the marks, the words, the lines of verse. The music teacher looked, in particular, at some notes of music, and both interested themselves in the initials. 'Look,' said the man of business, 'here is one shouting out a curse, and here is a line of verse lamenting in a way that could only be called self-indulgent by most people. Unrhyming of course. That's always easier to do, isn't it? You can say almost anything if it doesn't have to rhyme. And anonymous into the bargain. But who on earth are these people?' He bent again to examine the initials. 'As you know, I'm not up in the writers of the day,' he said, 'and none of these correspond to any writers I've ever heard of.'

'You're absolutely right,' said the other. 'These are obviously totally unknown persons – writers if you like, though unnamed and probably always will be. But therefore perfectly free to say whatever they want – anonymous and uninhibited. A chance in a million, you could say!'

It was nearing closing time. Again, there was a sudden, last-minute influx of people into the main room and a small crowd quickly surrounded the picture. Every sort of writing had now filled the entire square – rounded, childish writing, flowing, mannered script, close-written and highly cryptic scrawls, illiterate and ungrammatical lines followed by excessively well-phrased and elegant ones. Obscenities followed upon prayers and blessings upon curses. In between all these there were names, phone numbers, pleas for help, for love, money and jobs. Exclamation marks, question marks and inverted commas speckled the few spaces left, like some quiet, never-ending conversation going on in the background.

From a distance the canvas appeared to be covered with a meaningless network of crisscrossing lines and circles. Close up it became a rather beautiful work of art urgently executed by dozens of thwarted hands. But the new arrivals to the gallery fell back in disappointment and anger. They saw that they had been invited to write something here and pointed out the words in the corner – now almost obscured by all the rest. They came close and searched for spaces. Even the smallest space seemed to them better than nothing as they moved from side to side of the canvas to find where they might possibly fit themselves in. One man came in quickly behind the others and elbowed his way to the front. But a terrible wildness seized him as he recognised the chance there had been and now this chance crossed out. His disappointment appeared more spectacular than all the rest – to go further back in time, and to stretch further into the future.

'So there's not the smallest space even for my name!' he exclaimed, 'and God knows it's not a long one. But I had a lot to say. Even if I'd come half an hour sooner it would have been different. And if I'd come *first* – what a chance! I could have filled the entire square by myself. Well, even as a child, I was always too late. Did I ever see the fireworks? No, only the last sparks coming down in total darkness; the first and best jobs always filled before I got there; the only love who ever was or ever will be in my life gone years and years ago!'

The few now left around the picture looked non-plussed, while some were sympathetic and some annoyed at the effrontery of the words. 'The things you're talking about are all common enough. Don't we all know them?' said one. 'And, anyway, what can we do about it? We could only bring a great pot of white paint and go over the thing again. Maybe that's what you're asking for.' Others came forward to offer comfort – telling him what space and freedom might still be before him in life. But this was swept aside in contempt.

Now the last remnants of the crowd fell back again, this time in anger at themselves – some of them wondering whether they too had accepted too much emptiness, too much drudgery, too many rebuffs, reproaches and dismissals in their lives.

A great bell was clanging in some distant hall. It went on for a long time till only the shimmer of an echo was left through far-off corridors. One by one the people moved away from the wall and made for the door – each, before he left, looking over his shoulder at the picture and the man standing in front of it. An old official, almost due for retirement, had come up quietly behind this man.

'Will you write on it?' he asked. 'There's not much time. We're closing up in a few minutes. Will you write on the canvas?' he repeated.

'If I can find a space,' replied the other.

'Here is *one* space,' answered the warden, pointing to a small, round space dead in the centre of the canvas – a white space from which a few marks went out like waves or rays. 'Nobody has touched it,' he added.

'I wonder why,' said the last man waiting at the picture.

'Either they never noticed it or were looking for decent, bigger spaces to write on. Of course people can miss what's in the very centre in front of their eyes. On the other hand, they could be frightened of a circle. It's so complete that nobody wants to touch it. It's totally round like the moon or sun. Or maybe it's the wheel of fortune. Have you heard of that?'

'No, and never likely to, either,' said the last arrival, though his face had changed. He looked expectant. A last, quiet stroke of the bell sounded in the distance.

'For pity's sake, put something down quickly,' said the old man. 'You know how to write and draw, don't you? Anyway, it's the only place left. Maybe you think it's too small for your needs. You could just write your name, I suppose. Here's a thick pencil to help you.'

The last visitor to the gallery took the pencil and knelt at the canvas. He began to draw painstakingly and very

47

awkwardly, twisting his neck around to keep within the circle. He didn't write his name, but drew a small round face with round, enquiring eyes, a round mouth, round enough to cry, a round head and round curls on the head. It was a childish thing and had some idiotic hope about it.

'You've done very well,' said the official. They both stepped back to look.

'I'd never have believed it,' said the younger man. 'How did I not spot that small round space in the centre? What luck to find it!'

'But don't imagine it's a peaceful thing to be there,' said his companion. 'It's a whirlpool too. You know that?'

'Of course,' said the other, handing back the pencil. 'But then, I've been in a whirlpool all my life. I thought that was how everyone lived – inside or on the very edge of a whirlpool. Well, if I'm sucked down I'm sucked down, and that's all there is to it.'

'We're too late for the main door,' said the old man, taking him by the elbow. 'It will be closed and bolted. We can still manage it by the back exit. Do you mind? It's a bit hard to find your way into the middle of town by this particular exit. You'll just have to be wildly off-centre and possibly very late for whatever you're aiming at. But I'll accompany you down here, of course. I know all the twists and turns.'

Together they went down into the subterranean passages of the dead, silent gallery.

Counter Movements

'I see,' said the young woman suddenly after a long silence. 'Yes, I think I've got it at last.'

'Are you sure?' said her partner, giving her a rapid glance.

It was Saturday night – usually the best time of the week in the restaurant. People sat longer and seemed more relaxed. For many of them the next day would be free. Not all were relaxed, however. Some were tense, expecting crises of one kind or another.

The man and the woman were sitting side by side on high stools at a crowded counter. There was a long wall mirror behind the counter and two doors through which waiters went in and out of the kitchens, carrying trays of dishes and glasses. This was a feat needing great acrobatic skill. Sometimes they had to give the door a cautious kick with the point of a shoe or a sharp shove with an elbow. Then, for an instant, the scene inside the kitchen could be glimpsed as a perpetual dance. There were the sudden, bare-armed gestures, a flash of lifted lids through veils of steam, the flourish of coloured towels, or, when the tempo changed, came the slower, smoother bending down to ovens, and a balanced, tip-toe reaching towards high shelves. For this split second on the open slit of the door the diners at their tables craned eagerly as if from the poorer side-seats at the ballet.

51

'Yes, of course I'm sure,' said the girl to the young man, 'but better tell me again,' she added quickly. 'I don't want to forget the moment you're gone. I suppose you really *are* going?'

'Oh, we're not going through all *that* again, are we?' he said.

'Of course not. I mean are you going for good? What a phrase!' she added. 'For good! It's good for you, of course. Still, go on. Tell me again how I ought to manage.'

'As I said, you've got to start living your own life again,' said the man. 'Hour by hour and minute by minute. Lots of people learn to do it. You can get through everything that way. It's actually the way to make life longer too. And it's simple, though some of the greatest people have tried it – the mystics and the geniuses and even people who've only one day to live. It makes life worthwhile, you see, if you think of every minute as it goes by. Some people can do it with seconds, but I can only manage minutes myself.'

'Never mind,' said the girl. 'You're doing very well, as it is. How many minutes are there in a day, by the way?'

'That has nothing to do with it,' he said. 'What I'm talking about is the quality of living. You see, there's no use staring into the future and looking back at the past. All that's useless – a waste of energy. You have to grasp each moment, even the bad ones. Take it and crush it before it hurts you. Of course, it's hard at first. It's like grasping a nettle.'

'Oh I see it now, of course,' said the girl. 'It's the old stinging business all over again. Right then. Are you going?'

'I have to. We've been saying goodbye all day.' The girl agreed. She was very young, but the world seemed already echoing with goodbyes. In their travels it had obviously been the first time and the last time for every-thing. This mountain, this person, the particular village, the hidden lake – these they would probably never see again. It was natural, of course. The same for everyone. There was no great drama attached to it, though every opera they had ever seen was full of stupendous, scene-shaking farewells and unbelievable, sobbing sorrows. It was laughable really. Yet as time went on she felt these last times more.

'Goodbye then,' she said, looking along the counter where plates were passing swiftly and hands were con-fidently gripping the salts and peppers, the knives and forks. Hands were holding hands under the ledge.

'Goodbye,' said the young man. He left briskly.

The sudden departure of this young man left her on the edge of such a fearful gap that she felt dizzy. Long years and deep hollows opened up before her. She would not see him again. She looked around for help.

'What is it, dear?' said the waiter who was mixing up red and green peppers behind the counter. 'Is there anything you need? I see the dressing has travelled up to the top again. That bottle keeps getting stuck. People pay well for food in here of course. It really scares them when things go out of sight, I can tell you. So has the evening gone well for you?'

'My friend who left a moment ago kept talking about nettles.'

'But he's absolutely right,' said the waiter. 'They can be used in salads if they're well cooked. And in soups too. Common enough in the old days. Picked in the lanes when they were young and green. Trouble was you'd have to gather armfuls to make it worthwhile – piles and piles of fresh green ones. But today, what with the car fumes, anti-pest sprays, poisons for moles, rabbits and God knows what else, you wouldn't know what your nettles had soaked up – fresh green ones or whatever.'

'It's the stinging bit that interests my friend,' said the girl. 'He goes around grasping them and encouraging everyone else to do the same so they'll get well and truly stung. Oh, my God!'

'The thing is,' said the man, looking away for a second, 'they tend to lose their fresh colour when they're boiled. Go dark like spinach. But you haven't even begun your salad, have you? The dressing was coming down but it's got stuck again between that couple up there. That's worse. Everything gets stuck between *them*. That's love, I suppose. Pepper and salt and even vinegar – they all get stuck. Though it's a shame to mention vinegar along with people in love. Time enough for vinegar!'

The girl turned her head and looked down the counter at a stout-looking pair. 'They're not all that young, are they?'

'Careful, dear,' said the waiter. 'Ages aren't spoken about tonight. No ages and no weights. Saturday's age-less and weightless night. To tell you the honest truth, romance or no romance, Saturday's *got* to bring the money in. We've got to live and eat the same as others, haven't we? Just a moment,' he added, pressing a sharp elbow on the door of the kitchen, 'I'm going behind to have a look at the curry – extra hot, extra spicy and juicy on Saturdays, of course.'

The salad oil was sliding down the counter just as he came back. 'So this is it,' murmured the girl, grasping the slippery bottle. 'This is what I must start with to set myself up.'

'Don't vex yourself,' said the waiter. 'Just a drop or

two at a time. Again, it's rather a special line we make for Saturdays.'

'I don't suppose *you* can afford to be saying goodbye all the time,' said the girl. 'You can't be thinking of last times in your work, I mean.'

'You're dead right, we can't,' he replied. 'Naturally we send them off with a friendly goodbye at the end of the evening. But no. I never mention first or last times. Can't afford to in this business. There's competition up and down the street.'

'You know,' said the girl, 'what I was talking about was the absolutely final time of everything – plays, meals, walks, talks – everything!'

'I think I know what you're getting at,' said the salad man, 'but, curiously enough, it's a fact that just as many folk are *hoping* for the last time of something. You must have heard them. We hear it every night around the tables: "I hope to God it's the last time I'll ever set eyes on that selfish young devil;" "the last time I'll ever let myself in for a crappy play like that;" "for that ghastly bus-tour"; "that horrific dance". Only the other evening this woman said to her friend as I was removing her plate: "It's the last time I'll ever eat their prawns. I daresay I'll be up with them all night and down with them most of tomorrow too." So just remember that. For all the eyes-out crying over last times, as you call them, there's another lot desperately crying out for them. Thankfully there's this balance in everything – first times, last times, beginnings and endings – or we'd all be going round the bend.'

Again he disappeared behind the counter to the kitchen. The girl held up the bottle of oil and looked steadily through it for a moment or two. The place now appeared in a golden, viscous fluid – a wavering displacement of plates, glasses, fruits and bottles along the counter. The whole restaurant took on a tidal, under-sea appearance, forcing the slim white pillars around the walls to bend disconcertingly as if an earthquake had started up under the waves, while diners bulged and shrank and waved dissolving glasses through the yellow oil.

The girl saw the salad waiter appear suddenly again – his dark head a bobbing, bacchanal shape between artificial bunches of blue grapes hanging from the mirror.

'But don't imagine,' she said as if there'd been no interval in their talk, 'don't imagine that I won't get over it quickly. It's not like that. After all, it isn't a tragedy.'

'Of course it isn't,' he agreed.

'I was simply trying to explain,' she went on, 'that he reminds me of all the last times, the edges of things, even the precipices, the traps and gaps and those hidden holes you tread on without noticing. He could have warned me about all that. Instead of which . . . '

The man at the counter was making a curling froth of crisp lettuce in a blue bowl, adding thin circles of pale green cucumber, purple beetroot and thick discs of white and yellow egg. On this he laid twists of lemon rind and in the centre squeezed a rosette of thick white cheese from a tube.

'Instead of which . . . ' he prompted her, while keeping an eye on the nearby, noisy table where someone was shaking a napkin at him for attention. He grimaced at this as if coming upon some unexpectedly sour smell from the fresh salad.

'Instead of which,' said the girl, 'he set me, like some old schoolmaster, this awful, endless task of living every moment to the full until you die. He said you've got to feel them, taste them, chew them, stare at them. But on your own, of course. The point is that every single moment is a new one, and whatever happens, you've got to love it. Do you see?'

'Does he do it himself?' the waiter asked. 'I mean, does he do all that heavy chewing, swallowing, and so on? Does he have his own teeth, by the way? It sounds as if he's going to need them.' He was now tossing a mixture of green and yellow peppers in a white bowl.

'He didn't talk about his teeth,' said the girl. 'He just advises people and leaves them to get on with it. He's very good on advice.'

'So he's advising as he waves goodbye,' said the waiter. 'He must be always waving, I suppose.'

'But very gracefully, of course,' she said. 'That was the first thing I noticed. A graceful person.'

The man blew out his cheeks. 'Living *every* moment, did he say? That's a tall order. As for advice, I offer it myself when I'm around the tables, but strictly about the menus. Obviously they don't always take it. Or if they do they may not agree with it, or even worse, it doesn't agree with them. Look at that lot out there still waving their napkins as if I'd just stepped out of Buckingham Palace. What they really want is to get their knives into me for something or other. Naturally it's for something that's been put in or left off their plates. Would you believe it, I had one lot last week who found a cherry tucked away inside their steak and kidney? Unexpected, of course, but none the worse for that, you'd think. But oh no, they were perfectionists. They knew it was never meant to be in there – this cherry. And they're paying for perfection, or call it peace of mind. One cherry amongst five, you see. It could cause argument and strife. You couldn't divide a lovely thing like that. You'd never believe what happens in here.

The sweetest thing, the smallest thing can cause a riot that could really blow the place up.'

He moved up the counter where a small pool of red wine had been spilled. This he wiped off with a swipe of a snowy napkin before attending to the unruly table and finally disappearing to the kitchen.

He was away for some time before returning with a clean napkin over his arm and holding between his hands a great bowl of rice which he placed on a side table and started mixing, raising his elbows high and rhythmically, with two long forks held lightly between his fingers like the slim batons of some percussion player. His eyelids were lowered, but now and then his black eyes stole a measured glance towards nearby tables or along the counter from side to side, and even occasionally shot a look at the ceiling where ruby lights vibrated on their long chains whenever a new crowd pushed through the door from the windswept street. The girl watched him from a distance. Now he was quick and graceful as a dancer, bending his head to answer questions from the newcomers or curling his hand behind his ear to listen. Now and then he swung round from his bowl, snapped his fingers in the air and walked rapidly away to draw the attention of the slow, pale youths working away clumsily at the other end. Once more he went to the kitchen. When he came back he stopped beside the girl and leant on the counter, chin in hand. 'So he said that, did he?' he murmured. 'Every minute is a tough thing to expect any person to get through quietly. The trouble is that every now and then there's one so flat, so heartless, you think you'll never make it to the next one, far less the next hour or day.'

'Yet you always do?' said the girl.

'Well, I suppose I do. Anyway I've *got* to, whatever happens. This is my job, isn't it? I make my living here.'

'Well, how *do* you get through?'

'I'm telling you, I don't know any more than anyone else. Every minute is a new one, of course. You can have a different outlook every minute if you want to.'

'There's probably another way,' said the girl, taking up the bottle of salad oil again and staring through it. 'I mean the melting way,' she said. 'Letting everything melt and float gently past. There are no sharp edges, no breaks. Everything changes into – well, I don't know exactly – a kind of golden fluid. Very comforting, of course.'

'But I don't advise it,' said the salad waiter. 'Really I don't. I don't go in for the oily, floating bit in cooking and never have done. So I don't go in for it in my life either if I can help it. Personally I go for the crisp, the sharp and the well cut. You should see my cooking knives. I wouldn't think of leaving them about. Too many drifting, floating, unskilled staff around. Just take a look at those two young wimps up there, poor things. They seem to melt, to float away as you look at them. Believe it or not, one was greasing engines before he came my way. Now he's buttering neeps and carrots. The other was making hulking great cheese and meat sandwiches for workmen at a city take-away. Now I'm landed with both of them and they've nothing but girls and dancing on their minds. Can't get away quick enough when the shutters go down.'

Someone near his side of the room was calling: 'Are they free-range?'

'Eggs, I suppose,' said the waiter, 'or rather, chickens.' He strode out between the tables and came back. 'Chickens!' he pronounced. 'Free-range. I agree absolutely. Wouldn't have anything else in the place but free-range eggs. But it makes me wonder too. Would you say that man of yours was a free-ranger? From what

59

you tell me it certainly sounds like it. Makes them feel romantic and dashing, you see – always dashing for someone else before they're too old and have to start the year-counting. They're always first to give the good advice, of course.'

He was beckoned to a table on the right. He reached it almost in one leap, but not before calling back: 'Wait there for just one minute!' That was easy. She had so many minutes now. They were marked ahead of her, black and clearly spaced like figures on a huge timepiece. The waiter was in the centre of the floor, writing out an order, his notebook held close to his face. It was a long order and he wrote, intent and serious, with now and then an ecstatic cry as if following a dictate from some poet of the stomach juices. Finally he finished with a flourish. His concentration changed to a radiant smile. He left the table and made for the kitchens where the Italian family – the brothers and sisters, their wives and husbands, and even a grandmother and grandfather in the background – all played interchangeable roles.

It was the brothers who did much of the cooking and who discussed the choice of menu with their clients. This discussion was the main flavouring of the first course – a discussion often strong, sometimes hot, but never overdone. It was the sisters, for the most part, who brought desserts to the table and offered their advice. The fruit alone was often described in detail – the fruit as it had been taken off the tree – its summer colour and its fragrance somehow preserved even in the midst of winter. If an accompaniment to the fruit was asked for, it was never sweet or bland. It was the true companion – there only to bring out the flavour, the fragrance and the colour of these unusual fruits, ripened under a different sun. On this particular evening two grandmothers were washing up most of the time while keeping their eyes on the whole kitchen and giving shrill orders over their shoulders. There was a grandfather singing softly to himself while stirring pans. At intervals he sampled various unusual wines, holding them up to the light, shaking his head or nodding as he sipped.

The young waiter was a long time before appearing again in the restaurant. When he did, he made his entrance through a jingling, beaded curtain at the far end of the counter, raising his arms high to part the lines of silvery beads, like a water-sprite through a sparkling shower – surveying, at the same instant, his audience. Few people saw his entrance, for nothing could be further from a seeing, listening company than this one. These were pure eaters – demanding and hungry ones at that. For some minutes after settling to the meal, few had eyes for anything but the plates before them. Critical or appreciative eyes they had, and occasionally angry ones. Some were staring at the bits of food on the end of forks with the curiosity of collectors given an unusually suspect or rare piece to examine. The waiter was distributing more baskets of rolls along the counter. He reached the girl again. 'Well, how is it going? To find the knack of living every minute you have to learn to use the eyes. It's a marvellous cure for the heart.'

'I was using them all right,' said the girl. 'I was watching your entrance there. Are all Italians such actors?' His eyes flashed her a look of triumphant vanity.

'Don't imagine I'm all Italian. Not at all. One of my grandmothers is as Scottish as you are. The Scottish influence is a very sound, sensible one for people like us.'

'Do you have to make it sound such a damp, depressing one,' she said, 'like a freezing mist coming down over a sunny valley?'

'No, no, not like that at all. I'll admit the whole

British scene was very strange at first. Occasionally I've seen long-married couples sitting here, talking incredibly politely together: "I wonder if I might trouble you for the sauce, my dear? Oh no, don't bother. I can reach it myself." Well, just when you're wondering how they ever managed to get into bed together, you find they've made three or four children – even, by some miracle of God, five or six.'

'What you're describing about the polite talk may be British all right,' said the girl, 'but it sounds more like the English than the Scots.'

'Oh, so you like to divide them so strictly. You're a Nationalist, are you?'

'Well. I have a pride in my own country,' she said.

'The whole world's divided enough as it is,' said the man. 'The world needs Internationalists, people who can stroll across borders without shouting about themselves.'

'Look,' said the girl, 'I haven't explained myself properly.' She was getting ready to leave and the waiter was helping her with her coat.

'You never will,' he said. 'I've heard it all before. You hear everything over and over again in a place like this, and over the drinks as often as not. Ad nauseam. Naturally they have to go outside if they're going to throw up or throw things around in here. Quarrelling's second nature to us, of course. But in our country we like our fights outside in the open air and preferably on balconies. We like to shout and kick the chairs around. But personally I wouldn't care for a stand up fight or an unexploded bomb in this restaurant.' He accompanied her to the door, glancing over his shoulder on the way. 'Do you see that table back there, snapping fingers at me? Snapping fingers means trouble about the bill. So I have to go. I was lucky to have met you.'

'And I to meet you,' the girl replied.

'And anyone who comes here will be lucky with the food,' he said. 'A salad is not a simple thing. Remember my salad. Forget *me*, if you like.'

'Never,' said the girl.

'Then we are lucky. We can remember one another.'

In an instant they had both turned aside – he toward the table of finger-snappers and the girl into the revolving door, which, though she entered quickly, held her momentarily in the serene dancing motion of a perfect pirouette.

The Man Who Wanted to Smell Books

This was the time when every book in the world had been put on tape, when long ago every catalogue in every library could be read from hundreds of flickering screens which quickly settled down into a steady blue and green twilight shade, or at times a purple, violet and pink the colour of rainbows. The library which had once been a murky, mysterious place was fun at last. It was a place of games, movement and excitement. The change not only made the whole thing as colourful as a film show – it was also a tremendous help to everyone. No reader had to get his hands dirty searching along dusty shelves. There was no need to question and pester the librarian from morning till night. All twisting stairs and dank corners where intruders could lurk unseen had been demolished. Gone also were those dark cellars where people had eaten their sandwiches, made love, written their own books, meditated, slept and even occasionally died. Nowadays it was no longer necessary to lug awkward holdalls, briefcases and carrier bags. The heavy books were gone. The age of the Easy Reader was in. So also of the Happy Librarian.

Naturally there must always be someone who wants to spoil everything, who begins to look backwards instead of forwards. His head is forever twisted the wrong way round like the odd man out in a well-drilled regiment. Such persons have to be brought to heel in one way or another. For those with happy memories, or any memories at all, for that matter, are enemies of progress. Such a man was Charlie Syson who – while standing in an immaculate and streamlined library, strung with glittering tubes and wires, shining boxes and rainbow-coloured screens – remarked that he wanted to smell books again. He politely voiced this wish to a young girl standing by a table. She looked frightened at first, then agitated, then, as he hung about, moved nearer to her colleague and replied:

'I'm sorry, but you've come to the wrong place. You will never smell a book again here. I doubt if you'll smell one in any decent library now. All that sort of thing was done away with years ago. I've heard them talked about, of course – those smelly books. I believe you had to wash your hands after touching them in case you caught something. Most of them had those dark grey, brown and black covers so you could never really tell what was inside. Oh yes, my grandparents remember them. Sometimes they used to prop them up at mealtimes against a milk jug, poor old souls. Hygiene was scarcely thought of in those days. So I'm sorry, I can't help you about smelling books. But we still do have talks about them from time to time in this library, though people aren't very interested in the subject, I'm afraid. So there are always lots of tickets left over for these meetings if you care to apply for them.'

'But it wasn't *only* the smell,' said Syson, going back to his opening bid. 'I liked to feel them too. Some of them were rough, hard, even lumpy on the outside. Others were plump, padded and soft. And there was something thrilling too about the difference between the outside and the inside. The pages were either thick and grainy or smooth and silky. They could be yellow-

brown or pale brown, pure white or creamy-white.'
The two librarians exchanged a glance and looked
around to see whether the head of the place was near.
They realised whom they were speaking to now. They
were speaking to the Sensual Reader and, what was
worse, an elderly sensualist at that. 'But it's true,' said
the man. 'You couldn't tell what they were really like.
Well, what is anything *really* like – man, woman or
book? Yes, they were often black, brown and grey, but
even that dingy disguise appealed to me, if only for the
surprise when you opened them up. I liked to stroke
my fingers down the centre of a book before I started
to read. It is best with two fingers – the third and the
index, for example. Though naturally you can do it any
way you want.'

'Nobody does that sort of thing in here,' said the first
girl quickly. 'We deal with corners, edges, and flat, clean
surfaces. And everything is absolutely open and above
board. You are perfectly free to look around if you care
to.'

'Thanks, but I can see everything at a glance,' said
the old reader. 'That's the amazing thing – this seeing
everything at a glance, yet actually seeing nothing at all,
nothing but flashes and reflections, moving lights and
blinking coloured dots. It's mesmerising. It's a brilliant
idea!' He was thoughtful for a moment and went on:
'But don't think I was remembering only the old black
and brown books. Not at all. When I knew it, this
library occasionally got the brand new books as well.
They were so new that when you opened them for the
first time they gave a strange creak, a cry of pain – or
perhaps it was pleasure – at being discovered by an
ardent reader. In this way I established a kind of relation-
ship with the writer.' Their visitor looked about him.
'Obviously you are very far from your writers in here,

and a great deal better too, I daresay – uneasy, touchy creatures that they are! Vain, shy, irritable, inarticulate, unpredictable and uncompanionable. Yes indeed. How much better to file them away in boxes and on screens.'

'Oh I see you know a good deal about writers,' said one of the girls more cordially. 'What was your own job then?'

'I've been an addict of print as long as I can remember. I was a compositor in the old days. I suppose that gave me a head start. Naturally I miss the books. I miss the shelves. Even half-empty shelves were moving to me – those where the books stood alone and apart after the others had gone, like separated friends communicating only through empty space.'

'And I was told there were others,' said the librarian, 'so tightly packed you could hardly draw one out without breaking a finger joint.'

'Yes, and I liked to give those grimy old books an occasional airing,' the visitor replied. 'Those ancient histories of dentistry, yellowing like old teeth, the musty clerical biographies and the volumes of hell-fire sermons, surveys of streets and houses long since demolished. How close yet isolated they were!'

One of the girls whom Syson had first approached stepped forward now.

'You don't find the screens rather exciting?' she asked. He looked around him. It was true the eerie screens seemed related to the space and movement of a universe rather than to a city library. The man had to admit that this was their attraction. The flickering green and white lines against an unearthly blue were like no known writing. With this script one was meant to speak and write to dead friends, consult oracles or angels, make one's pact with the devil or with God, as well as learning languages, taking advice from the doctor and dictating the details of the funeral. These screens had the mesmeric quality of all glass, thick and thin – the glass of telescopes, microscopes and crystals. The magic of hieroglyphics was here, and of undiscovered numbers and letters. Perhaps, the old reader thought, the whole world would soon become a gigantic screen on which one might decipher stories and histories of the cosmos – a huge white blank like those monstrous drive-in TV screens on which limousines, skyscrapers and gigantic, mouthing faces loom out suddenly from a lonely American background of forests, mountains and prairies.

But the girl was speaking again. 'Don't think we don't understand you. As I said, most of us had parents and grandparents who were great readers in their time. I personally had grandparents who had a load of books they carted from place to place, lugged reverently from house to house. No, I haven't smelled one myself but I have an old photo of my grandmother holding a book very close to her face. No doubt she was doing just that. Or was she hiding?'

'Yes, yes,' the visitor admitted, 'it was possible to hide the face or even the whole head in a book. For complete privacy one simply shifted the book sideways or up and down. Every reader knew the trick, and no-one held it against the other. Not many places around here to hide, are there?'

The girl looked rather uneasily around the place. She was slim, but it was true there were few places to hide face or body. Here all things had been arranged in space as economically as possible. Most objects were sharply rectangular. Amongst them were flat containers holding hundreds of flat slides and round containers holding stacks of thin, round discs.

'I've no need to hide,' said the girl. 'And anyway I still can't understand what you have against cleanness, against neatness. The world's getting smaller every day, more crowded, and the time shorter. Think of the new space created here, the extra time. Can't you understand the miracle of the new techniques?'

'Talking about miracles,' said Charlie Syson, 'have you ever been round a paper-mill?'

'Never,' said the girl, closing her lips about the word as if paper was not and never had been a concern of her profession.

'Luckily,' said her visitor, 'I once had a friend who worked in such a mill when he was young. And very thankful I am I saw it before all those places disappeared for ever. This was one of the last to go. I saw the paper being made – the best paper, I'm talking about, not the fibrous newspaper stuff, the woody end of the trade. No, this was the best. I've seen the rags come down in lorryloads from factories and shops. White cuts and strips from shirts, blouses, sheets and tablecloths, some coloureds amongst them, all sorted into piles. Then every snip had to be beaten, pulped with water, pressed and squeezed dry.'

'And then?' said the girl.

'Beaten again,' said the man. 'Beaten. Then squeezed again, squeezed and squeezed dry.'

The girl sat down on the one chair near the counter. She murmured that she had been standing for a long time in the hot library, and that paper, as compared with light, colour and speed, was not something she could ever become excited about.

'I simply wanted you to feel how people laboured over the centuries to make this finer and finer paper,' said Syson, 'how they polished and refined it till it had the gloss of ivory or silk. They were proud of the stuff. Paper had always a royal history. It was a fit present for a king, emperor or pope. It was in monastery libraries, in palaces, even in ancient tombs. I myself when I left this paper-mill, was given a wad of fresh-cut paper, fit for a king.'

'What kind was it?' the girl asked.

'Writing paper. A great packet of the first-class stuff.'

'So you write endless letters?'

'None at all if I can help it. A postcard's all I've ever managed for years.'

'There, you see!' she exclaimed. 'All this praise for paper. Yet you've no use for it yourself.'

'Certainly not for letters. But it's not writing I'm talking about. It's reading. And by the way, what did you do with all the books? You must have been in the pulping business yourself. Or maybe you burned them.'

'A mixture of both,' the girl replied. 'But please don't imagine that we haven't saved a few. Of course we have. And people are perfectly welcome to look at them whenever they wish to.'

'You mean you can take me to them right now?' said the reader.

'Just wait for a moment. I'll come back in five minutes and take you down.'

Syson wandered about for a while, hands in pockets, in case he should disturb the zigzagging script on the screens. Yet he knew nothing could be disturbed here. The pattern was set, frenzied yet rigid. It was he himself who was madly disturbed by the brilliant predictability of the place, the cleanness, the smoothness, the demented mathematical order of every machine. Once in a while he raised his eyes to the window and saw – almost with disbelief – a cloud go past, expanding, dissolving, saw a bird, a leaf fly up, wayward and restless on the wind. The girl came back five minutes later. 'I'm ready now,' she said, 'if you'd like to come down to the basement where we keep some of the old books.'

The old reader went slowly down with her. Now he almost dreaded to see the old loves of his youth. Indeed, he dreaded to see how much they might have changed, how he might have changed himself. The girl herself seemed nervous, talking in a whisper as if careful not to awaken some dangerous creature from its lair. She opened the door a crack and he looked in, sweating a little in the warm, burial atmosphere of the place. He was aware he was peering into a Tutankhamen's tomb of buried books. 'You can smell them now, if that's what you want,' said the girl over her shoulder as she went in. She bent down to a shelf where there were some large volumes. Syson lifted the heaviest in both hands and studied its hard, dark grey cover with the black lettering.

'Do you know what this is?' he asked.

'No, as a matter of fact I've never known,' she replied. 'Never wanted to know either. Is it an art treasure?' She opened it up gingerly. 'It doesn't look like one, does it? No colour, and the writing's nothing special, neither the writing nor the paper.'

'It's ordinary print and paper,' said the visitor. 'And it's a book on insects – every insect in the world from A to Z.'

'Oh, what a disappointment for you!' cried the girl with genuine pity.

'No,' said Syson. 'It's a privilege to hold one of the surviving books – and very well preserved it is too, no mark or tear.'

'Just how it managed to survive, I've no idea,' said the girl. 'I daresay the cover was stronger than most, or maybe it's the dry atmosphere down here. All the same, I'm still sorry the first thing you laid hands on should be a book on insects, of all things.'

'What better thing to find,' said the reader. 'Aren't insects themselves the great survivors?'

'We haven't much time to worry about survival here,' said the girl. 'And the smallest flea could hardly survive upstairs. There's not a speck of dust to hide behind. But tell me about your insects.'

'To put it plainly,' her visitor replied, 'if we blow ourselves off the planet along with every living creature, those wiry insects will keep going. Perhaps a few to start with, then more and more as time goes on, till they take over the entire globe – a buzzing, hissing, crawling globe.'

'Could we go up soon?' said the girl. 'It's stuffy down here and there isn't a lot more to see.'

'No more treasures?' Syson asked.

'Very few. Some old pens, I believe. A typewriter, a curious reading-lamp that can bend its head any way you want, a magnifying glass, an ancient pair of spectacles, some rather sinister little bottles of white poison – the kind of thing the ancient scribes tipped their arrows with – Tipp-Ex it was called.'

Syson drew out a few other books. There was a small pencil-written diary of some early polar expedition. He pressed the thin book against his chest until the warmth of his body penetrated the pages. Through the cover he felt his heart knocking against his hand. 'Feel that,' he said to the girl. 'No book was made simply from sheets of paper. There's blood and a beating heart in there.'

She laid her hand cautiously on the cover, saying again, 'Could we go up now?'

Upstairs the other girl at the counter was waiting. 'Has the gentleman seen what he wanted to see?' she asked. 'Did he look at the books? Did he have time to study the old writing-desk with the ink stains, the revolving deskchair, the bookcases with the shelves? If you're making a private museum,' she said to the reader, 'we'd be very pleased to consider selling them.'

'No, no, they're safe enough here,' said Charlie Syson. 'You must keep them. I'm getting old. If I took them, who knows what might happen to them when I die. I have no children, you understand.'

'But take something,' said the librarian. 'Take something – seeing you're so interested. What about an unusual pen? A Biro it was called. Or I believe we could find a real old pen with ink in a bottle if we looked in the basement cupboards.' A pen and ink arrived for Syson and he opened the visitors' book. There were other signings on this page. Amongst a list of names he noticed many symbols – flowers, birds, beetles, animals and trees. These were the signs of the oldest visitors who had almost forgotten how to write their names.

Charlie Syson turned over a leaf and signed boldly on a smooth, new page. Something told him this was the last time he would write his name on a good piece of paper again.

'And if you don't mind putting your occupation too,' said the librarian politely. Beside his name Syson wrote: READER (ext.).

'What does ext. stand for?' asked the librarian. 'Is it a foreign degree or an honorary term?'

'Not a degree,' Syson replied, 'and certainly no honour. Ext. stands for extinct.'

'Why, Mr Syson, we are all readers here!' she exclaimed. All around her, as if to confirm this, the green and blue lines flickered from every screen, while pulsing red and green dots and a rainbow of reflections streamed from distant corners of the room. There was a throbbing, a ticking, a humming of smooth-running instruments.

'I can add "a reader of the paper pages of books", if

76

the meaning isn't clear,' the visitor said, 'or even "the good-smelling pages of books".'

'No, that's all right,' said the librarian quickly. 'We understand perfectly what you mean.'

At the same time, when Charlie Syson took his eyes from the machines he realised that the handling of paper and ancient books here had created a warmer feeling towards himself. It was not that they were hard on him, not critical. He was to be treated as a child, regressed beyond cure. But a child – even one with a total lack of adjustment – must still be cherished, set right and kept going for years and years in the better world.

It was nearly closing time and the two young assistants opened the heavy, outer door. As their visitor stepped into the street a strong wind struck him. While he was momentarily sent staggering it came to him as a pleasant shock that nobody so far had managed to tidy and control this particular part of the planet. A few old scraps of paper flew towards his feet like birds towards a bird-lover. He picked one up as it brushed his ankle. It appeared to be torn from an ancient 'thankyou' letter, but the paper was tough, good quality stuff such as he'd described not long before. Moreover, it was inscribed in very clear pen and ink. 'It may be some time, but I will come again,' the scrap of sentence confidently predicted. Charlie Syson held it up and waved.

From the doorway the neat librarians waved back, before fastening the door firmly upon the dust and grit, the peel and paper, the petals, fluff and feathers of the runaway natural world.

Obstruction on the Line

There is a point on the coast, coming down in wintertime from the north, when the distant lights of Edinburgh come suddenly into view. There is still a long distance to go, of course, before the train will swing in a slow, smooth curve on to the Forth Bridge, but on a dark night these distant lights have a reviving effect on tired travellers. Those still looking out begin to think of welcoming warmth, food, drink, and a comfortable bed. The buffet has probably been closed down long ago, empty cartons and beer cans are rolling around on the tables and one or two people are sound asleep with their heads on their arms. The papers and magazines have all been read and tossed aside in the aisle. One by one the voluble strangers fall silent. The babies begin to howl in earnest.

One cold night, on just such a journey, and in sight of the far-off lights, it was, then, a fearful thing to feel the train very gradually slowing down. There was one great, final jolt before it stopped. After a moment of absolute silence, in which some made out the cry of a bird from a distant wood, the steps of the guard were heard coming along the platform. 'A short halt . . . ' came the announcement through the loudspeaker. 'Very much regret . . . a slight obstruction on the line . . . nothing serious . . . should be removed very quickly.' The passengers could hardly believe their ears. That such a thing could happen in shining distance of everything human, everything warm and familiar! They glanced at one another, wondering what they could possibly do now. The food was finished, the papers read. All sources of conversation had been used up long ago, and the whole place was in chaos. Their immediate future had suddenly vanished. It was now a case of living in a shabby, worn-out past.

The guard was questioned as to how long it would take. Ten minutes became twenty. Half an hour was apologetically brought forward. Finally a statement came over that anyone who wished to get out for a short time 'to stretch the legs' should do so now. At first there was a great lack of enthusiasm for leg-stretching, until a few started to get up and others came from behind. A pale girl with a red, woollen cap had joined them. She carried a very young baby in her arms – a good, silent baby, they were thankful to note. No-one had seen her before, as she'd come from far down the train with the rest. Once she bent and asked politely of those on either side: 'Where is this?' A foolish question, some thought, for it was nowhere. Several times she nodded as if a place had been named, and once she murmured: 'I know it.' The group looking out from the carriage door could see only a rough siding, a vandalised railway hut, and an ancient cottage – no more than a pile of old stones and a couple of window frames, with a bleak bit of moor behind. It was now that the girl turned back for a moment and greatly embarrassed several matronly women who were still sitting near her by asking if they would hold her baby. This would have seemed not unnatural, of course, but to one she said: 'Will you look after him carefully? He will be safe with you.'

'I'll take him for a *moment*,' said one woman cautiously. He was a stiff, delicate, silent little thing in a soft white shawl. But why safe? Isn't a baby always safe with its own mother? They were relieved when she took him back again.

'That's a pretty sad kind of a mother,' an oilman muttered, glancing back. 'It's my guess the father, whoever he was, made off in double quick time.'

The group stood silently, still staring out at the empty place. That was the worst of it. If they were to get out, there would be nothing to see, not a bench to sit on, not a roof for shelter, nowhere to walk, and no lights.

'Still, there's only one thing to do,' said a businessman's wife. 'We really ought to get out, as that man said, and keep the circulation going.'

'It's when they're to get the train going that worries me,' said her husband. 'Never mind the circulation.'

Seven people stepped down stiffly from the train – the businessman and his wife, the oilman from Aberdeen, a middle-aged teacher, Emma Paterson, who had been sitting beside him, the girl with the baby, and two young sailors from Stonehaven. A few began to feel sorry for the girl with the baby. She looked very pale and cold and murmured that she was eager to get home. She'd been cold for so long, she said.

'So have we all,' said the red-faced businessman with a grim laugh. 'And what's more, the whisky disappeared well over an hour ago.' But outside it was colder than they had expected. 'Will your baby be all right?' said the teacher.

'Oh yes, he's well wrapped up,' said the girl, looking down and touching his eyelids lightly with one finger. It was true the baby was wrapped from head to foot, motionless and unprotesting as a stiff little doll.

'All the same, I wouldn't stay out too long if I were you,' said the other woman.

'We're used to it,' said the girl quietly. She was polite,

but too distant, the woman thought. It was hard to reach her. The teacher quickened her steps to make up on the businessman and his wife. They'd seemed heavy-going inside the train, but could prove better company in an empty landscape than this girl. The oilman and the two sailors followed close behind.

The seven people walked along the platform for a bit and stopped abruptly as they reached the front of the train. A huge mound of red clay and earth with a bit of wall behind had been washed down by last night's rain and was piled up on the line. On one side was a long, narrow trench. The teacher stared down the length of the dark trench and shivered violently.

'You're cold,' said one of the sailors, putting his hand on her arm.'

'Freezing!' she replied and turned to walk back. Three men were coming up with shovels over their shoulders. At that moment there was an outlandish hooting from the train, calling the travellers in. It came to the minds of one or two how lonely that blast might sound if one woke in the night in some nearby house. But there were no houses here. No welcoming window was alight. Good news awaited them as they boarded the train. 'We'll be going in ten minutes or so,' said a lawyer, waving some papers above his head. He had sat tight from the beginning of the disturbance and managed a good forty minutes' work on his briefs. 'We're all here now. Thank heaven we can get on our way at last!'

'No, no, we're *not* all here!' cried the teacher, Emma. 'There's the girl in the red beret still to come. For God's sake don't let it go without her!'

The oilman got up at once and went carefully through the entire train, coming back to his seat with some satisfaction, having found an unread newspaper in the aisle. The two sailors rose together, went briskly up and down the platform from end to end and got in again, one remarking that it was beginning to pour out there, and just because they were seamen it didn't mean they had to get soaked to the skin. Very disturbed now, the teacher called the guard, who went outside himself for a long time, came in again and went through the train slowly, methodically, and seat by seat, asking questions as he went. He came back again to where the teacher and the oilman sat together, smiling and well-pleased with himself. 'Well, you can stop your worrying. Your young lady with the red hat is sitting down there, as happy as you please. As a matter of fact she's coming up to borrow a magazine and you'll see her for yourself.' The woman came down almost at once and picked up the cast-off magazine. It seemed at first as if Emma Paterson hardly dared to look at her as she went past the table. Then she glanced at her head. Sure enough the woman was wearing a red hat, but it was a wide-brimmed straw hat that might have looked good at a midsummer wedding. The teacher stared in despair and terror at this hat and went off to find the guard. This was *not* the person she'd been talking about, she said. No, nothing like her. There followed a reasonable discussion about styles of hats and then a more desperate one about different shades of red. Finally there came a severe warning from the guard about the absolute necessity of getting the train started. There was talk of time-tables. It was very late already. He had found the lady she wanted. What more could he do? Connections had been disrupted for miles along the line. How often he'd known people make mistakes in recognising others on a journey. He saw it every day. It was all part of the job on railways. People didn't even recognise their own baggage, let alone another's headgear. Even as he spoke, the train gave a grinding lurch, and they were off.

'Where is the girl with the baby?' said the woman once again. But this time it was no more than a whisper, scarcely heard by those across the aisle. She had become very pale and was at last persuaded to take her seat, where she sat with her head bowed, pressing one hand hard against her lips.

'Don't worry,' said one of the sailors from behind. 'I don't think we'll be late at all. They usually go as fast as possible after a hold-up.' It was true. The train was now tearing along through the darkness. The speed seemed to cheer everyone enormously. Emma was now staring out of the window, seeing the twisted black branches suddenly outlined by light and a few wild creatures rushing away from the train into the dark. The window panes were black. Now and then she saw her face reflected against a background of empty fields. From an isolated cottage one yellow window shone, and near at hand a few sheep were huddled at a hedge against the rain. It seemed she was flying through the loneliest stretch of country she had ever seen – though it was a familiar enough part to her. Yet this time it was different. In the foreground, on glass, silvered with drops of rain, floated her unfamiliar moon-white face with tragic, tearful eyes.

They were nearing home at last. The train was approaching the bridge and the oilman was pointing to a lit-up rig very far out. 'Well, I wouldn't want to be out there,' she murmured, thinking that the black sea where rigs might founder was not much lonelier than the dark fields where lost souls wander. The man began to talk of his work on the rigs a year or so back.

'It's a world of its own,' he said, 'and not a bit easy to describe. How can you describe it when you can't compare it to anything else in the world? It's not a liner, and it's certainly not a floating palace. You're out there with dozens and dozens of other men. Yet you're on your own. Something to do with the sea, I suppose. The accidents that happen there aren't like anything happening on land.' He decided she wasn't a very rewarding person to talk to. She kept turning her head and staring up the empty aisle of the train. Then she would look blankly out beyond him to the distant rig, as if she were staring at a child's toy floating in a bathtub.

'Accidents!' he repeated. She looked away, of course, as they always did. Didn't want to know. 'Broken legs and deep wounds — that's normal,' he said. 'Two of my mates were swept overboard and drowned. Another was knocked unconscious by a bit of swinging metal. Yes, of course the worst cases go ashore by helicopter. But by that time it could be four hours' wait — two for the thing to come and two hours back. Anything can happen. Often they're beyond help. They could be dead. Some very heavy stuff is loaded on by crane,' he said after a moment. 'That's to say, you can have a great load of steel pipes swinging overhead in a stormy sea. If you do happen to fall into the North Sea, that's the end. It's not like a sunny dip in the Med., you know. Oil,' he said after a time. 'Some people think you scoop it up like oil from a frying pan. In fact, you wouldn't believe how deep the stuff is down there, and in some of the oldest rocks on earth.'

The woman listened to all this patiently as if waiting for his voice to cease so that she could give her whole attention to something else. 'It's a terrible life out there in some ways,' said the oilman, 'but I missed it when I finally came off. Couldn't settle down again to the silence and the safety, after all those months.' At last the woman leant her elbows on the table, turned her head towards him and asked:

87

'You *did* see her, didn't you? You did see the girl in the red cap with the baby?'

'Yes, I saw her,' he replied at once to quieten her, and simply because the way she stared at him so fixedly embarrassed him. She seemed very slightly relieved. 'But I think some people didn't,' she said. 'And I couldn't bear to think she might have been left behind all alone.'

'No need to worry whether they've seen her or not,' said the oilman. 'People never pay much attention to one another on trains. All got their minds fixed on getting home. Nothing else matters. She'll turn up all right when we get there in twenty minutes or so. And don't forget,' he added, 'maybe she was in the loo for a long, long time. Babies need changing, after all. Not such an easy thing to manage in a temperamental train like this.' Emma Paterson agreed with him, but listlessly, as if, long ago, she'd run through every possible explanation for a vanishing.

The two now turned away from the window and looked across to the others. Once over the bridge, everyone had come to life again. Some were already pulling down cases and putting their coats on, while others were looking for buried gloves or searching for the small, lost gifts they were hoping to take home.

The train came in hardly fifteen minutes late. Everybody rushed along the platform looking neither to right nor left, except for the woman in the red straw hat who looked back once at the teacher as she went past her and said irascibly: 'I heard something about red hats back there. Is there anything *wrong* with mine?'

'Far from it,' Emma replied, 'far from it.' The other gave a slight toss of her head and went briskly on towards the barrier.

Nothing could depress the hurrying travellers now,

not even the longest taxi queue. At the end of it they
visualised home, fire and food. Very soon they'd be
telling of the train hold-up, the empty shelves of the
buffet and the cold walk along the platform. There are
always some people, of course, who can't take it, they'd
say. There was this woman who'd made an awful fuss
about someone – about some girl in a red cap, it might
have been. Or a baby or something. It was difficult to
hear, and we can't remember now. It's so wonderful to
be back at last, to forget all about it. What was the
hold-up? Nothing at all, really. Only a mound of earth
and a sort of hole in the ground. It took only minutes
to clear, of course, but it seemed like hours.

Since then the teacher had made that particular journey many times again. Her favourite cousins lived in
the north and she visited them as often as she could.
The return journey was always the same. The train
would seem to gather more and more speed when nearing home. On each occasion the passengers woke up,
becoming exceedingly cheerful and talkative as they
thundered along under the great spars of the bridge and
saw the lights of the city beginning to spread out around
them.

On none of these homeward journeys had there ever
been another obstruction on the line. Yet on every one
of them there was a particular point – still a long distance
from the bridge – at which this woman experienced a
heavy obstruction in her throat, like the aching lump
which gradually grows in order to suppress a violent
bout of weeping. Yet she knew this aching loss and grief
was not her own. It had been hidden in the memory of
another woman living beside the north and southbound
route long years ago – a memory buried deep and most
despairingly laid in a dark, narrow house, before vanishing for ever in the distant past.

The Hairdresser

9 '*I*'m very fond of that young brother of yours. He's such an innocent,' said the hairdresser suddenly.

Jo, the elder brother, suffered an unfamiliar pang of jealousy. But he quickly replied: 'Yes, he's got a nice round head, my brother has.'

'Oh, it's nothing to do with head-shapes,' said the hairdresser as he parted the boy's hair to one side and made ready for the wash.

'Well, it's the colour then,' said Jo. 'It's always been blond and shiny like my mother's. And it lies so smooth and flat across his head.'

'No, it's not the colour either,' said the hairdresser. 'He just happens to be rather a sweet kid.'

Jo experienced a surge of total pity for himself as he heard these words. Unbelievably, for a second, he felt like bursting into tears. He stared doggedly ahead into the barber's mirror. He had rough black hair and sombre eyes. When troubled, his brow became darkly lined. He could scowl like an angry man. The hairdresser was dark too, but he was tall and handsome and wore a smart grey suit with a striped purple and scarlet tie, plus handkerchief to match in his breast pocket. His hands were firm as he stroked hair into place, as he shook out the warm towels and deftly tucked them in round the necks of his customers. Nobody could call his place a first-class establishment. It was on the very edge of the city and consisted of two fair-sized rooms – one where he worked and the adjoining one where customers, mostly elderly, waited. Young people came here too, of course, but those with money travelled further. The older men came for a quick shave and trim, the women for a crimp, a cut or a tint on a greying head. The hairdresser was good at his work and a kind man. He complimented all comers, young or old, and made the whitest heads shine like bridal satin.

Today, before tackling Jo's head, the hairdresser fussed about for some time further up the shop, softly brushing up the scattered mixtures of hair he'd cut earlier, the brown, black, blonde, red and grey, then swabbing round the basins and checking to see how far down the coloured liquid was in rows of bottles on the ledge above. Finally he looked through the glass panel into the other room to see how many were still waiting. He said nothing as he moved about.

At last he came back to the boy and stood looking down at him silently. He saw that Jo was totally downcast, that he sat, his head drooping, staring at the towel under his folded hands. The hairdresser bent low over him.

'Mind *you*,' the man murmured so quietly that his breath scarcely stirred a hair of Jo's head, 'that same little brother of yours is a real hard little customer when he's got a mind to be. I'd say you had the sweeter temperament, by a long way.' Jo felt a sharp, painful pleasure deep within his chest, mixed with the slightest touch of shame at the word 'sweeter'. He said nothing but held up a corner of the towel against his cheek which had turned pink.

Now the hairdresser was preparing for the wash. Gently he pressed Jo's head down towards the basin and started up the lather. Soon the boy's head was puffy with white foam. When at last he raised it the hairdresser pinched up the stiff foam in pointed tufts and peaks around the ears. This gave the head in the mirror a grotesque and mildly diabolic appearance. The hairdresser laughed and with one swift swipe of his hand smoothed the white foam softly over again, making the head look round, placid and innocent as a melting snowman. Now he started to rinse, spraying on the hot and cold, and finally enveloping the boy's head in a hot, rough towel. First he rubbed Jo's head vigorously and then clasped it between his hands as if bestowing comfort or forgiveness – Jo had no idea for what. He imagined it might have been because of his jealousy, or even forgiveness for his unusual silence that afternoon. He had not talked or laughed much. Nor had he responded to the childish foam joke. He was no longer a child, and he felt some impending sorrow in the air. The hairdresser gave the towelled head a couple of gentle pats and turned on the dryer. But before the hair was quite dry he started to cut – first chopping off the longer locks and then, after spraying the sides again, holding the flat hair between two fingers to make a perfectly straight cut above the ears. Now he started to trim the back, gently lifting the hair and clipping up with comb and fine scissors from nape to crown. Finally he snipped with great precision close around each ear, like a mason pointing a rough, stone block with his sharpest instrument. Carefully he dried the head completely before stepping back to examine his work.

'So now we'd better have some music while I finish tidying the place,' he said, bringing across a small record player and putting on a tape. 'The ending,' he explained, while the plaintive notes of a single violin soared slowly, tentatively, up through the storm and silences of a great orchestra. The hairdresser made no move at all to finish tidying, but sat listening intently, his arms behind his head, long legs stretched out. At last the violin climbed slowly, sorrowfully through all the rest, up to one last high note – one note of final, killing pain. The boy imagined how all the strings of the orchestra were now gently lowering their bows into one long, vibrating silence. Even the hall might perhaps sustain this final silence for some time. It would vibrate through the bodies, through the minds of the audience as they left the place. He could not imagine talk.

The silence inside the shop lasted until a van hideously hooted in the street outside. The hairdresser remarked evenly: 'That young violinist was a great friend of mine. Not long after that performance he left for another country. Exactly one year later, when I was preparing to visit him, he fell ill and died. That was the worst sorrow I ever knew. I hope you will never go through anything of that kind yourself.'

Jo was silent. It seemed that the human voice could have little or nothing to say following the emotion of a violin. He wondered if he himself could ever learn to speak in some totally new and fervent way. It was too late now, of course. Even the hairdresser had not managed to learn, nor had the solitary old people chatting in the next room. As for the tightly married couples, they talked mostly to one another. There was no easy way into their secret and sacred sects.

At last the hairdresser got to his feet. He was pale and admitted that it was nearly always cold in this room, in this town, in this country. 'I don't know whether I mentioned it last time I saw you,' he began in rather a stilted voice, 'but I'll soon be moving to other premises down south – in Brighton, to be exact.' He paused and added in a voice even more strained and formal: 'The particular place where I'll be working will be a great deal more cheerful than this. I shall be in the midst of rather different company. I shall be with artists, musicians and actors, and with several friends of mine who are still there where I belong. Where I *did* belong, I mean. Of course I should never have left.'

The boy in the chair listened and nodded coolly enough to all this, keeping his eyes steadily on the man's face. This, he'd noticed, was how mature people were supposed to take a really bad bit of news, neither frowning, flinching or fidgeting, not even speaking or interrupting in any way, not batting an eyelid until the whole thing was said and done. And a perfectly expressionless face was obviously more attractive to most than a hideously contorted one.

He had known the hairdresser for quite a while – since he'd arrived in the place nearly three years before. Since then the man had told him a bit about his training and his work, and was pleased to show him all the implements and secrets of his trade. There were various types of scissors, blunt ones and sharp, for instance, for different cuts and even for different parts of the head. He had explained what he could do with long hair and with short hair, and how he experimented with colour. As time went on he spoke to Jo as an equal in all experience. 'But all that is nothing,' he once said, talking of the changes he could make upon heads. 'Some men and women wish to change themselves *totally*. This is more serious. Naturally the old wish to be younger, and the young older. There are tragedies and comedies inside this shop. Sometimes the older ones have fallen in love with young men and women, and occasionally the youngest – far too young to be taken seriously – fall for those much older than themselves. None of them, young or old, are concerned with their minds, their

morals, their lasting happiness or their reason. No doubt
because of this they do not go to a doctor, a clergyman,
a psychiatrist or even to their best friend. Believe it or
not, they come to me. They trust me, you see, not to
laugh, not to cry, not to scold or advise – but simply to
make them look younger or older, as the case may be.
But always, whatever else, better-looking. I am not a
magician, of course,' the hairdresser had added, glancing rather vainly into the mirror, 'but I have always
known, since I was your age, a good deal about human
feeling. I daresay it shows somewhere. Not on my face,
I hope. I can't afford to embarrass customers. No, not
on my face, but maybe it's the way I handle those unruly
heads that come my way. When I was young I wished
to be a sculptor, then a doctor, then some sort of con-
juror in a music hall – a cheap and garish hall, for choice.
I felt more comfortable going downhill in those days,
as long as there was money to be made.'

'Seeing we've been talking about young and old,' the
hairdresser had said one day, 'we'd better remember the
middle-aged. They are thought to be easy. I mean it's
widely believed they've come to a sort of plateau where
they rest for a short while – supposedly peacefully –
until the next storm comes sweeping round and lays
them flat on their backs.' He made a sweeping gesture
with a large comb as if combing down the wild, whistling plateau grass. Jo had thought of his father and
mother who had obviously missed any chance of the
peaceful plateau far back along the way. Years ago it
had sunk below the horizon.

'The middle-aged are often realists – to use a hateful
word,' the man went on. 'They are not looking for
dramatic changes. The changes I do in here are tempor-
ary, but spectacular – and mostly for the young. Some
of them may last only a few days: time for a dinner date,

time for a dance, time for the briefest love affair. I like such changes. They are exciting. People smile and laugh when they see these transformations. They think all their life may change between washings. Well, sometimes it does, and good luck to them!'

'At any rate, *you* are lucky,' Jo had said that day. 'People here must like you a lot.'

'Not always,' the hairdresser had replied. 'Some people like me, naturally. Some distrust me. A few may even hate me.'

Today, Jo looked back on all the earlier talks. But he particularly recalled the conversation on ages – the old, the middle-aged and the young.

'How old are *you*?' he asked suddenly.

'What a question!' exclaimed the hairdresser. 'I am forty-six.'

'You once told me the middle-aged aren't looking for huge changes,' said Jo accusingly. 'And yet you're going miles away to be with people you hardly know.'

'But I told you,' said the man, 'many of them are still my friends. I wish to go back before I'm too old. Anyway, I'm off as soon as possible. The other town has a lot going for it, you know, and I don't just mean the sun and the summer crowds. There are those dazzling white cliffs, endless walks, restaurants galore, and you should see the shore in winter. The noise of those stones in a storm! Some day you must come and see me when I get fully established.' His voice faded a little on the last word and he glanced at the boy. He noticed that he was holding up a very small, square towel before his face. Silently, without looking at him, the hairdresser handed him another. It was the biggest towel in the place and enveloped him like a beachrobe. Again the man moved off and spent a long time pottering about the end of the room, pressing new pins into posters of hot-haired girls where they'd come unstuck, and putting the bottles of dye, brilliantine, bleach and conditioner on to a high shelf, the combs, curlers and scissors into a long box. When he returned to the main shop he found Jo sitting quietly, his hands on the arms of his chair.

'Well, that's a lot tidier, isn't it?' said the hairdresser cheerfully.

The boy looked round and stared with red eyes. 'It's still an awful mess,' he said. 'Why did you never put up more shelves?'

'It always seemed too late,' the man replied. 'And now the shop will probably be sold to a fishmonger or someone like that. They wouldn't need many shelves, would they?'

'I suppose not,' said Jo, looking mournfully bored. 'They usually keep the fish packed in long boxes with slabs of ice.'

'Well, it's funny how everything changes in a flash,' said the man. 'I once saw a dress shop change into a butcher's in a couple of days. Whole dripping, bloody beasts hanging from hooks where two days before it had been pink and blue evening dresses with sequin straps. Well, what would we do without change? How boring life would be.'

'So you knew long ago you'd be going,' said the boy.

'I wouldn't say long ago. But six months back I'd almost decided.'

'I still don't understand. Whatever you say, most people liked you.'

The hairdresser looked through the glass panel at the other room where the elderly women were still patiently waiting.

'Oh, I'm tolerated,' he said. 'No-one *particularly* likes me.'

'My parents like you,' said Jo. 'They often wonder what you're doing here.'

'That's just the point. What *am* I doing here? It isn't a place that exactly shows its liking, is it? Don't get up just yet. I've still got to brush this grand collar of yours. Hairs stick like mad to velvet. Now, that's a fine shape of head you've got – a fine, brainy shape of head,' he murmured, softly whiffling round the collar and up and down the shorn nape. 'What did you say you were going to be?'

'I never said,' the boy replied. 'You never asked before. I may be a lawyer like my father and grand-father.' There was no indication that the hairdresser was still listening, but after a moment he removed the large towel from the boy's shoulders with an exaggerated obeisance like a stage footman removing the cloak of a prince. Then he accompanied him down through the waiting room to the threshold of the outside door.

'So it's goodbye, then, my dear young friend,' he said, looking casually across to the lights of moving cars, 'and don't forget to visit me some day in the not too distant future. Only a good day's journey by train.'

At the word 'future' the rattle of stones on the far-off Brighton beach became almost inaudible. The glittering white cliffs were so remote their tops were scarcely vis-ible in a swirling sea mist. From the road the boy looked back once, and the hairdresser waved. It was a friendly wave, but casual. So casual, so friendly, so gracious was the gesture in the doorway that he might have been – from some totally inaccessible distance – finally, deter-minedly, motioning the boy away.

Waiting

'I shall never, never be a waiter,' said Gabriele one night as she stood with her mother in part of the silent restaurant which was also their home.

'Well, that's one thing you'll never need to worry about,' her mother replied. 'There *are* no women waiters. Only waitresses.'

'But then, I will never be a waitress either,' said the girl. 'I never want to wait. Waiting looks a miserable, miserable thing to be doing night after night.'

'Waiting isn't necessarily doing,' her mother replied. 'Sometimes it is simply standing still.'

Unfortunately this was true. It seemed unfair that Gabriele's father, Signor Dominick Gentile – an eager and industrious man – had often to stand still, simply waiting in his own, newly-opened Edinburgh restaurant. Naturally he and his wife would be busy long before customers came in. But customers seldom came in, and often for half an evening the place would be almost empty. Dominick was a forty-six-year-old Italian from Genoa who had come to Edinburgh from his native city only a few months previously. Twelve years before, however, he had been in Scotland for several months while visiting cousins, long settled there since the war. During this short visit he had met and married a Scottish woman, Jeanette, who – apart from her other attractions – was an excellent cook. She had

returned with him to Italy. But after a decade, an ideal-
ised memory of their love and of various distant friends
they had made in the other land began to obsess Dominick. His wife, a less romantic person, said simply that
she had become homesick. Before long they were back
in Scotland with their daughter Gabriele, a charming
ten-year-old, black-haired, and with the vivid gestures
of her father, yet at the same time pink, white, and
sensible like her mother. The couple had quickly settled
in a rather drab corner of the city and opened their
restaurant. It was very hard work. The meals were
always ready, however many or however few there
were to eat them. To keep expenses down there were
only three or four helping about the place. Jeanette did
all the cooking, assisted by a boy who peeled the vegetables and washed up. A woman helped with the cleaning twice a week. There was one young waitress who
was an asset to the place, being pretty, helpful, cour-
teous to customers and a friend for Gabriele. But as time
went on in the silent place, she began to show a lack of
confidence even in the way she put the plates down or
hooked up the coats on the coat-rack. She was, in fact,
beginning to wonder how long her job could continue
in the half-empty room. When winter came she would
put her arms around the half-dozen big coats for a
moment before hooking them up, as if to press and
warm herself against the only persons who were likely
to come in that night. Once or twice Dominick had
spoken rather severely about this. He said he didn't care
to see a nice girl hugging a coat or rubbing her cheek
against a jacket of fur or leather. Certain people might
get a totally wrong idea of her character. Meanwhile he
had put a big placard on the pavement in front of the
restaurant on its east-facing corner. It was the wrong
sort of placard. They had not counted on gales and rain.

Strangely enough Dominick had never spent a whole season here, while his wife, her mind still on certain Italian autumns, had clean forgotten other weather. The poster, nailed to the placard and advertising the delights of the restaurant, was stripped off in the gale and the board itself was blown down. One evening both stand and placard were blown out into the street and under the wheels of a passing car. The car was not damaged and no-one was hurt. It was Dominick who was deeply hurt, for the incident was noted in an evening paper, plus the name of the café. Dominick was in black depression for weeks. It was the disgrace. He believed his place – already patronised by few – would now be shunned by all. There was not even a placard now. Only a poster stuck to the window, difficult to read in the dim light.

As a young man in Genoa, Dominick had been under-waiter in a small, crowded restaurant in the best part of the city. He had learnt all his skills from his father. He knew the trick of carrying things, of putting down a variety of piping hot dishes neither too quickly nor too slowly, of holding up rare wines to the light before pouring them with a steady hand; of shaking out stiff, lily-folded napkins above the diners' heads without disturbing a hair. He had been particularly skilled in the way he could pass quickly and quietly between the close, crowded tables of his father's restaurant so that neither his cuff, his elbow, or the corner of the cloth over his arm would touch the cuffs and the elbows of his customers or the edge of the cloths on the tables. At that time he had always been good-natured, happy to describe and demonstrate the food and drink to natives and foreigners alike. He was a handsome man, rather heavy, with strong, expressive features which could quickly fall into melancholy. Nowadays, though he was

melancholy a great deal of the time, he never dropped
for a moment his exalted pride in being a waiter. He
still walked as carefully through his almost empty restaurant as he'd done at his father's place – one elbow
draped with a napkin held closely to his side, as if he
were moving with difficulty through an impossibly
crowded room. As he finally turned away from some
solitary couple he would give a graceful, circular bow
which seemed to include at least a dozen other satisfied
guests – all ghost-guests of those who should have been
around. For the miserable fact was that few people had
seemed to notice his door. He had tried many things.
He had installed music. His choice of opera, in this case,
was not an absolutely happy one. From a box high up
on the wall Madame Butterfly also waited interminably
throughout each evening, often weeping hopelessly and
staring from the window, sometimes on her knees
speaking to her child, but always waiting, waiting for
the absent lover.

Occasionally some couple would ask him about his
own city, Genoa. While Butterfly's passionate voice rose
and fell in accompaniment, he would tell them of the
stalls in its narrow streets where, amongst green leaves,
the close-packed rows of fishes lay curled, tail to mouth,
along with huge trays packed with oysters and mussels.
Here were pyramids of green and yellow vegetables,
knocked over in passing, while the noise of bargaining
and scolding across the stalls was matched only by the
singing, shouting and scolding coming from open
windows above, where women were leaning, their faces
half obscured by sheets, pillowslips and pyjamas drying
on the crisscrossing lines between. Sometimes they
would look back from brilliant sunshine into the darkness of the room where an instrument might be playing
or a child calling. Life was lived outside here, the Italian

would go on, and this was the great port of the seafaring world where ship-building was still the great trade. It was the travellers' port. They knew, of course, that Christopher Columbus had been born there? Oh, how Dominick longed to mention Columbus to all those Americans who came to Edinburgh and who appeared to claim the great sailor for themselves! But so far the Americans had not come to his restaurant. Genoa, he explained again, was a city of flowers and fruit – olives, vines, chestnut trees and orange orchards. From being very subdued and keeping his voice down and his hands still, Dominick became excited and his voice grew loud. He took them through the market again, building up the pyramids of fruit and vegetables with his hands, showing with his curved forefingers and his thumbs the mouth-to-tail arrangement of the fish. And the food in the restaurants there! Again he lowered his voice to a whisper as he mentioned the Genoese speciality which was there on his menu in his handwriting. He pointed it out: *Trenette col pesto*. Perhaps they knew it already. If so, he apologised to his customers for telling them. It was spaghetti served with a sauce made with garlic, basil, cheese from Sardinia, and olive oil. Dominick stopped. This was an unusually quiet part of the city. He was listening to the cries of Madame Butterfly, slowly diminishing in despair. In the street one or two cars went by, and the discreet footsteps of people returning from the city centre to villas on the outskirts. Dominick gently clapped his palms against his ears: 'In Genoa there is much noise, much talk, much crying,' he said. 'And not only Christopher Columbus is born here, but Paganini also,' he explained softly to the table as he walked away.

Being not yet too squeezed for money, Dominick's life would have seemed bearable for a time if it had not

been for his large family at the other end – in Genoa.
This was the worst of it, though once it had seemed the
best. For he loved his family. Yet what a cross they
were to him now! His father and mother, his many
brothers and sisters and their husbands, his aunts,
uncles, cousins, nephews and nieces! They expected the
greatest things from him, demanded the highest
achievement and insisted on hearing it. And what was
worse, he told them the greatest things – writing regularly and rapturously of his happy and successful life in
Scotland, the growth of the restaurant, the well-fitted
kitchens, the pictures, the music, the flowers, and above
all, the crowds – the noisy, happy, satisfied crowds at
his tables. God and all the saints would surely forgive
him! His parents were getting old. He, their eldest, was
the favourite. No-one had expected more, given him
more than they had. Such a spectacular failure as his, far
off in another country, would surely shorten their lives.

These letters home he would write grimly, dutifully,
with his wife gasping over his shoulder. 'Be careful what
you are doing. One day they will come,' she had said.

'Yes, of course they will come,' he'd replied. 'Let
them. By that time we'll be making a big success.' His
wife was sensible, down-to-earth, and as honest as only
really difficult women can be.

'But is that the *truth*?' she asked.

'It *will* be the truth one day,' he said.

His mother, Signora Gentile, was a devoted woman
and the mainstay of her large household in Genoa. Her
faith was great. Her cooking, shopping, cleaning, her
long years of childbearing – all had been done to the
glory of God. Yet even on her knees she looked a proud
woman, still beautiful, straight-backed and very dignified in her fine black dress. She was proud of her family,
proud of her husband's position. She had never deigned

to bring artificial flowers into the church. This spring she brought two big bunches of fresh lilies and three expensive red roses. She herself seldom asked the Mother of God for things. More often what she said could sound like commiseration or even like the advice of one anxious mother to another. Nevertheless, this time she mentioned how extraordinarily well her son, Dominick, was doing, how successful and popular he was in his work. The Queen of Heaven in her sparkling crown – one large, marble lily hidden tactfully in the fold of her robe, looked down at her impassively, merely the hint of a smile denting the corners of her lips.

One day the shattering letter arrived from Italy. Dominick's mother wrote that, as he had once mentioned a visit, they would gladly take up the invitation. As many of them as could make it were coming across for the second anniversary of the opening of his splendid restaurant. No plan was to be in the least disturbed for them. They would arrive from the station by taxi at exactly eight-thirty, God willing. They were taking the cheapest, shortest package tour in the book. It would simply give them one night to be in his place, and the following day they would have a little time to see how Dominick's beautiful and only child had grown, and then a glimpse or two of the famous city before going back. Jeanette read of her beautiful and only child with some resentment. She was keenly aware of having married into a family who believed that the woman who did not try for at least half a dozen beautiful children could hardly be called a woman, far less a genuine mother. Nevertheless she put the feeling aside in an attempt to rise to the family crisis – the most serious one in their lives. 'So what are they going to see when they arrive?' she asked. 'An empty restaurant. Oh yes,

I can make them a very good meal. But there will be no crowd but themselves to go with it. No racks of coats and hats, no noise, no laughing, no talk, and no singing except the everlasting crying from that box up there.'

They were at last forced to take in the fact that his father and mother, a brother, two sisters and their husbands would be arriving in four weeks on the evening of their second anniversary. There had always been too much free time in the restaurant, and now Dominick and his wife spent it talking, arguing and working out their plan. The idea came to Dominick as he was staring out one evening through his uncurtained windows. Occasionally people approached, looked into the empty place, glanced at the menu on the door and walked away. 'I am going to put another poster on that window,' said Dominick, two weeks before the arrival of his relatives.

'Yes, you've done that before,' replied his wife. 'It didn't work.'

'This one will work,' said Dominick. 'I know the human heart better than you do.' It was really the human stomach that he knew well. He spent many evenings working on the words and design of the poster. Ten days before the anniversary he stuck it on the window. It was large and Dominick had splashed it with colour. The letters were clear and big enough to be read from some distance away. 'THIS RESTAURANT,' it said, 'WELCOMES YOU TO ITS SECOND ANNIVERSARY DINNER on Oct. 19 at 7.30. THE MAIN COURSE (your own choice) IS FREE AND IS GIVEN WITH THE COMPLIMENTS OF DOMINICK AND HIS WIFE JEANETTE. We would be grateful for your punctuality.' During some days before the date people were seen to stop and approach the window, as usual, out of mild interest. They had seen the words: 'THIS RESTAURANT' and fully expected to see them followed by 'WILL SHORTLY BE CLOSING DOWN'. However, they remained pressed to the window for a long time, reading with closest interest – finally leaving, gesticulating and laughing incredulously while beckoning others to come up and see. This behaviour was very unusual at this particular corner and in this exceedingly undemonstrative street. Many others came up to read and left in the same manner. Two days before this special dinner a very large crowd arrived to read the poster. Naturally there was scepticism, much jostling and speculation. An unusual amount of elbowing and neck-craning was going on amongst those ladies and gentlemen who had never used their elbows in their lives and seldom stretched their necks. Determination and a discreetly disguised greed were the main expressions on the faces pressed to the windowpane.

The day before, Dominick and his wife were busier than they had ever been. More posters of Italy – its mountains, lakes and vineyards – were put up. And other cities, apart from Genoa, were there also. The spires, domes and fountains, the markets in the squares, the sculpture and the churches of Rome, Florence, Sienna and Venice glowed from the walls. But so as not to arouse any acrimony there were also some spectacular posters of Edinburgh and of the mountains, lochs and towns of Scotland. In only one thing Dominick was stubborn. He would not put up posters of the fish shops or fruit stalls of Edinburgh, refusing to believe that any shopkeeper of the city knew how to show the brilliant piles of fruit and vegetables as they should be shown. And as to the cold fish, limp and unadorned, staring with glassy eyes from their white trays! He was sorry.

Naturally not all arrangements could be works of art. But there it was. These were still his walls. He would put on them what he wished. As for the rest of the room, the white cloths were covered with leaves and flowers. The heavy, patterned plates, saucers and jugs, set upon squares of pink, white and blue napkins, resembled the table in still-life paintings. Matisse himself could not have arranged them better. From the early hours of the day itself Dominick and Jeanette were working in the kitchen, preparing the speciality of the house – the spaghetti with its aromatic sauce plus an excellent salad. Hors d'oeuvres, soups and sweets were not forgotten, as customers were expected to eat plentifully of the whole menu, seeing the place had been unbelievably generous with the main course. As the evening went on the strange dark corner of the street was transformed. Dominick had put a stronger bulb in his outside lamp and his wife had polished the step till it shone like Carrara marble. On the broad window ledge inside they had placed an outsize basket of green leaves covered with oranges and purple grapes. The great crowd arrived early. Yet something about the dignified figure of Dominick in the entrance prevented too much rush and jostling. But even so, some restraint was needed to ensure that people were moving in an orderly way through the narrow doors. Dominick's method of restraint was to stand quite still, smilingly supporting himself with one arm on the side of the door – the other was on his hip, swathed from wrist to elbow in a starched white napkin. The little waitress who had disappeared some weeks before had been brought back again. This time there were too many coats to hug and cuddle. Dominick himself took the women's coats and scarves, removing them with a tender pride as if he were uncovering some precious statue after years of dust and neglect. There was an unfamiliar geniality and excitement in the air. Tonight the passionate pleas of a rejected Japanese woman, far from depressing the company, seemed to break down the reserves of even the most repressed.

Soon every table was full, except for the large one in the centre which was reserved for seven persons. At a quarter past seven, while she was bringing in steaming platters of spaghetti from the kitchen, Jeanette stopped short and cried to Dominick, coming behind, 'For God's sake take down that poster! They'll be on us in an hour!' Dominick stripped down the window's notice and, for the first time, in its place, proudly hung up the black-lettered sign: 'FULL UP'. Then he regretfully closed the door on the expectant eyes peering in, indicating that, though the place was crowded out that night, it would be open to early-comers next evening and, he hoped, for many, many evenings to follow.

At eight-thirty punctually the seven members of his family arrived. Before going round to the house door at the side, they too paused momentarily at the windows, staring transfixed at the crowd inside. Signora Gentile threw up her arms in amazement at the sight, while her husband, dignified like his son, simply smiled proudly, at the same time making a deep bow to the whole room. Dominick's sisters, meantime, were wondering why, with all the produce of Italy at their disposal, their own husbands – both teachers – had never chosen the obvious way to make good in a very short time. Inside, everyone had been waiting to see who would take up the vacant seats in the centre. In fifteen minutes, not unaware of their importance, the party was making its way toward the table, lit with its seven fat candles. While Dominick bent to blow them out more than a month's worth of news was exchanged – an overflow too long even for letters – news of more distant relatives, of births, deaths and marriages, of old friends and new enemies, strange illnesses and miraculous cures, of the catastrophic break-up of business deals and the dirty scandals in political life. A history of the bitter vendettas of certain neighbours was worked over for the hundredth time and here and there a reconciliation was touched on with brooding incredulity. During this narration the party were being stared at like royalty. Soon they were being served like royalty. Signora Gentile wore a magnificent black silk dress, moulded to a stout but well-corseted figure. Over this was a stole of black lace, fringed with crimson. Jet earrings hung below hair smooth and shining as a black silk cap, lightly threaded here and there with white. In the knot at the nape of her neck she had twisted a red rose found amongst the left-over flowers of the kitchen. Nevertheless she was a woman with some feeling for her surroundings. After a quick glance round at other diners she quietly removed it and placed it in the flower jug on the table.

To all those within earshot the Signora introduced herself, her husband, her daughters, and her sons-in-law. She apologised for the many relations unable to come. She admitted one could not be always boasting about one's own. Yet they could see with their own eyes the cleverness and success of this, her eldest son, chef and owner of the restaurant. She made it clear that of course she had other worthy sons throughout Italy. Before long her son in Edinburgh would doubtless have many other fine children himself – success and plenty naturally going hand in hand. Like some great hostess, Signora Gentile seemed by her words to gather the whole room into her group, at the same time indicating that, rather than listening to her, they must go on with their excellent meal. Though most of the candles were burning down, the piles of fruit diminishing, and a few flowers wilting, colour, amiability and confidence, plus a warmth due only in part to the free, hot food, circulated throughout the place as she spoke. A great hunger was satisfied that night.

People went by the restaurant till all hours, forever turning aside to watch a bottle held up to the light, to follow the steaming plates passing or empty ones being taken away to be replaced by fruits and creams. From the faces at nearby tables these outsiders tried to imagine snatches of conversation, and through bursts of laughter heard from an open window-slit, tried to make out the jokes. Even from doubledeckers, stopping at traffic lights, people gazed down into the festive place, craning around to see what the platters held, while promising themselves a night out at the first opportunity. Cars slowed up to point out the restaurant to their passengers, noting its name and number. Towards midnight a few late vandals, hoping to put a stone through the window of a dark corner, were stopped in their tracks by the look of the place. An important person – if not an actual queen – appeared to be holding forth in the centre of a crowded room. There were several dark men in her company, fierce and protective, possibly armed to the teeth with more than table knives. The restaurant shone on into the early hours, its blue and rose lights flooding the wet pavement like the floating colours of some master's hand, stroking paint and prosperity lavishly, gratefully, on to a grey canvas.

Choirmaster

One day, out of the blue, it came to Sam, the choirmaster, that God must be very tired of people constantly flopping to the ground and begging for this and that. Rows of men, women and children on their knees – whispering, imploring, pleading, whether in song or prayer. What way was that to ask for anything? God, it was said, was all-powerful and could do anything on earth or in heaven. Heaven was an unknown quantity, of course. But, looking around the earth, people could see things had gone badly, drastically wrong. Drought and famine had ravished some lands more ferociously than others. The sickening stench of death rose from the hot earth, and from the baked mud of the riverbanks. Birth and death arrived suddenly together. Scarcely was there time to dispose of the afterbirth than the burial cloths were unwound. Gone were the days when any choir could sing cheerfully of the good seed being sown and scattered regularly by men and watered just as punctually by God. The eyes of all those in this land dried up in their sockets while staring at the terrible, brazen sky. At each dawn all the vessels in the place were brought out – the jugs, the pitchers, basins and baths in order to catch every drop of the miraculous, God-given liquid when it fell. No water fell. No water had fallen for weeks and months. Obviously, as the old choirmaster now believed, God must be weary of the bent knee and the humble, bowed head. Perhaps it was bold, abusive songs and outraged shouts He was hoping for, not the quiet, muttered prayer and the thanks which would make the lesser gods shrivel with shame. Was it not possible that God wished to be commanded for a change, not cajoled at all?

Sam had always been a lusty shouter himself. He had formed his choir as he travelled, and as he travelled continually, he gathered together a huge company of men, women and children from the remoter parts of the world. He picked his singers from the desperate and hungry, from the ill and even the dying, from people too weak to work and from some who had been almost beaten to the ground by servitude. He therefore knew that wherever they went in the world, his choir would be singing to companions in suffering; and so, whatever else it sounded like, whatever words or music were used – the song must ring true. His singers understood this, and if they were forced to compete with tornadoes, the pounding of huge waves, claps of thunder, the last rumblings of earthquake – the more they tried to rise to Sam's demands. It was true they had their own demands, but never for anything petty. Depending on what piece of land they were passing through, the men asked for what they imagined were the simple rights of every man. They demanded work, water, bread, decent huts and medicine. Occasionally they might pray to God for death. The women asked for all these as well as care and comfort for their children. Occasionally they might ask for fewer babies and sometimes even for more, as long as they still had milk to give them.

As time went on some desperate people asked if it were possible that God might be a little deaf on account of His great age. Perhaps He was no music-lover, in

spite of some talk of angelic choirs. Then the choirmaster saw that he would have his work cut out, teaching, explaining, reprimanding and generally dealing
with the strong emotions of his singers.

'Look,' he said one day to his hungry and unhappy
crowd. 'Please, if you can possibly help it, don't cry
when you're begging for anything. Begging's bad
enough, but begging *and* crying must make God feel
really mean. Do you want Him to feel mean?'

'Yes, I do,' said a blind old man with fly-encrusted
sores around his eyes and down his legs. His feet were
bound in grey bandages and he leant on a stick. It was
true he was on his last legs, yet might still live for a day
or so.

'No, I don't think *I* do,' said a gaunt-faced, middle-
aged woman with four small children behind her, two
others clutching at her cloak, and a bulge-eyed baby in
her arms. 'They are all beautiful,' she said, indicating
each child with a nod of her head, 'but will I have the
strength to love and feed them all?'

It was true that hundreds of people in the huge
choir had hardly enough strength to raise their voices.
A few could do nothing but lie on the ground and
wait for death for themselves and their children. This
would often come quickly. But a decent burial took
strength from the living and many died in the doing
of it.

Not everyone in the choir agreed with Sam's method
of singing loudly all the time with scarcely a break.

'Hadn't we better stop and listen once in a while?'
asked one old-fashioned believer. 'Wasn't there something about a still, small voice?'

'Yes, I've heard that, but I've always been against the
idea,' said the choirmaster. 'As long as we've got the
strength, we're here to sing, not to listen. Sure, people

want to join my choir for all kinds of reasons. They tell me they've got great voices, clear voices, that they can reach the highest notes and the lowest. And, naturally, people like that have ambitions to be the star singer. Or maybe they've no voice at all, but just want to get away from a plaguing family back home. Whatever they've come for, what help are they to a company like ours, especially if they're interested in small voices? Isn't it hard enough to get people to stand up straight and open their mouths?'

Yet for a time the old choirmaster did think of adding to his singers. And it was not only here that he looked. There were plenty of good voices back in his own country to which he returned for a short time. Many there had joined in processions and stood on platforms, for one cause or another. Groups with banners gathered outside hospitals, colleges and churches. Some he brought back to his choir, whether they had fine voices or not. He needed to make up for all he had lost through sickness or death. But he himself changed a great deal as he grew older. He had seen so much of horror, pain and misery in the land that the idea of singing songs of love or thanks for anything on earth seemed out of the question. Nowadays, outrage toward heaven was what he looked for in his singers – anything that gave force and fury to the human voice, his only rule being that they sing with chests out and heads flung back. Always they must be defiant, never suppliant.

Sam would have liked the suffering creatures of the earth to be heard in his choir – birds and animals as well as men. For he believed that many creatures might find more protection there than those outside who suffered the cruelty of human beings – the trap-setters, the cage-builders and the money-makers behind the bleeding hell of the slaughterhouses. Yet, on second thoughts, he decided to stick only to humans and allowed them to sing exactly as they pleased, whether in fear, pain, fury or sorrow. As long as they made a loud enough noise they might curse or weep as much as they liked. There was, he told them, no one God to cry to – or, if only one, He had obviously been created by all races of men, in all ages of Time, and out of every belief that had ever been attempted on earth. The choirmaster again reminded his singers that thanksgiving must sometimes be very tough on God. No doubt He might rather be bullied a bit, scolded, and even openly threatened for a change.

The choirmaster was growing old and tired. These days he was often hard put to vary the singing to every catastrophe. They came so thick and fast there was hardly time to draw breath before the next shattered the community; the flood and famine, dust and drought, disease and death, and all followed by endless questions: 'Why, why, why?' Then the hopeless non-answers. Finally silence.

But the old man kept on with his training. Above all, it was essential to teach his choir the loud and soft notes in the human voice. They had to sing as loud as possible to be heard through the landslides and earthquakes, or simply to alert the desperate inhabitants of lonely places that help was on the way. It also took great skill to teach them to change from the loudest possible crescendo to a sound so quiet that the cry of an infant or even the whisper of a dying child might be located under some mountain of rubble.

By this time the outrage choir was pretty well established, but one day the choirmaster – ever on the look out for likely singers – picked up another possible member. His company was passing a forest one evening when a young man appeared out of the darkness between two trees. The trees were tall, their broad jungle-leaves casting great shadows around the new-comer, giving the impression that he was delicate. This was an illusion. He was thin but sturdy with strong, muscular legs and large, workman's hands. He had the unusual attraction of a darkish brown skin and clear, blue eyes. It was hard to tell whether he came from the north, the south, the east or the west.

'I heard you coming a long way off,' he said. 'What sort of procession is it?'

'No procession at all,' Sam answered. 'This is a choir, and monstrously hard work it is too, dealing with an unruly crowd like this. But I'm not grumbling because that's exactly what I want them to be – unruly and complaining!'

'What are they complaining about?' the young man asked.

'Complaining's a poor word. I was wrong to use it,' replied the choirmaster. 'They're not girning or whingeing about some paltry thing, some petty grudge. Those who still have strength are shouting to high heaven about the hopelessness of this earth – the thirst, the hunger, the pain, the misery. Some are still singing quite sweetly, of course. Most are cursing.'

'Lord, but it must be a tough job leading a choir like that!' exclaimed the stranger.

'It certainly is. But one day I might get them to sing properly as well as shout. I confess it was I who worked them up. But still, it *is* supposed to be a choir, not only a furious rabble.'

'May I join your choir?' the young man asked.

'It all depends on the voice,' said the choirmaster.

'A tenor,' the other replied.

'Then I doubt if I can take you on,' said Sam. 'Tenors

tend to sing about sweetness, peace, love, harmony and the rest of it. All the things this world is almost totally lacking in. Myself, I believed in all that once. Not now, of course.'

'And I can sing solos,' the young man went on, as if not having heard the last remark.

'Sorry, but I never allow solo singing,' said the choirmaster firmly. 'Soloists always become vain, no matter how modest they seem to be at the start. They tend to be temperamental too, and before you know where you are, they're acting like spoilt children. There is this terrific silence whenever a tenor solo gets up to sing – you must have noticed that yourself – as if he were a prince or god or some such being. People can even fall in love with tenors before the last note's out. It all plays havoc with a well-trained choir, and this *is* a well-trained choir! Once they've settled down you'll hear them sing. And I've worked so hard with them. A good choir is my one real aim in life. As in every art it's a case of balance and gravity, if you like. We can't afford too much emotion.'

'Nevertheless, you need a hell of a lot of emotion to sing well,' said the young man. 'To put anything across at all – that's a lifetime's work. Anyway, you're certainly putting it over. There's no doubt it will reach this Almighty Person you're singing to.'

'You mean He has huge, listening ears as well as everything else?'

'Possibly,' said the other. 'I've never thought about His different parts.'

'Wherever He is, I seldom think about Him nowadays,' said the old choirmaster. 'He has allowed such fearful things to happen here. I can hardly bring myself to look up at all, far less utter a respectful word. I think I'd choke if I did. Yet I can still manage to train a good choir. Imagine that!'

'You're probably best to choke and have done with it,' the newcomer replied. 'And I like people who speak their minds. Myself, I'm not so fond of the meek as I was sometimes thought to be when I was young.'

'You certainly still look young enough to me!' exclaimed the choirmaster.

'No, no, I can scarcely remember what that was like. I think I never was really young at all.'

'Well, I'll let you join us for a bit,' said the older man, 'and we can judge what kind of voice you have. Naturally, I can't promise anything right now. A great many people have wanted to join, but the moment they find it's not a church outing with picnic included, they fall away at once.'

'I've no interest in church choirs myself, nor Sunday school picnics, for that matter,' the young man assured him.

So it turned out that this newcomer was allowed to practise with the rest. But the choirmaster knew he was taking a big risk. The choir itself was never too pleased with his rare, haphazard choice of new members. Moreover, it was no longer as straightforward as in the old days when the choirmaster had been full of optimism and simple belief. Nowadays any new recruits he chose for his choir were strangely mixed. Either they would show too little anger in their voices – falling back into the old, placating tone, or else they allowed out-of-hand fury to spoil the rhythm and tempo of the song.

Yet the old choirmaster didn't hurry his new member into song. He allowed him to find his feet before he even opened his mouth. The young man was simply encouraged to walk along with the choir for a while, not singing, but just chatting with them, finding out how much strength they could still summon up for practice, hearing how they could still manage to sing in harmony even while often hating one another's guts. Some would confess how deeply they resented what they'd heard of other choirs in the cities of the world – choirs used to all the perks of wealthy companies – applause that went on for hours with endless flower-throwing, plus banquets and bouquets and beautiful women. Many, in fact, were bitter that they'd ever met up with the old choirmaster who, for reasons of his own, had, early on, gathered them into this company where they now suffered the humiliation of becoming a crowd of travelling beggars under a one-time raving idealist who could offer no food, no water, no medicine and no comfort of any kind, while gradually letting his own hopes and beliefs peter out as the arid, blazing days went on. Sometimes he appeared unsteady on his feet as the starving inhabitants of each village pressed around him, trying to claw pity from his heart. Often, at night, he would wonder what would become of him if pity ever deserted him.

As for the choir, the reasons for their present suffering gradually became clear. Long ago, when Sam took over, he had forced them to sing – no, not merely to sing but to shout – loud and triumphantly about the Love of God. Love! The scorn, the fury, the disappointment and bitterness in their singing gradually grew to a raucous crescendo as they realised what they had walked into, unawares. And now, even the old choirmaster was dis-integrating before their eyes.

'So he's seen no more of this enormous love than we have!' they cried. 'This old man's taken us through deadly heat and freezing cold with nowhere to camp – through forests and deserts, all of us hungry and filthy as pariah dogs. He thinks we'll follow for the rest of our lives, like fools. Let's sing something different, so furiously blasphemous it will frighten the life out of him. Then we can run back to our homes, if there's still a home to run to. But where will our children be now? Will our husbands and wives have left long ago? They will curse us for leaving, then curse us for coming back! What a fix the old one has got us into! May he be damned!'

The new singer held up his hand. 'Wait!' he shouted. 'Don't forget your God gave you freedom – the freedom to come or to go, to turn good into bad and bad into good. But have you taken your freedom?'

Again the air was filled with furious muttering. More fierce cries and curses went up into the sky. 'There must be silence!' the young leading singer reminded them, 'or else the God will not hear that He is loved and forgiven!'

'Never! How we have suffered!' came shouts from every side. 'Where is this love? He had no love. Now we have none ourselves!'

The great trees whistled and creaked in accord. Hissing came through the dripping leaves. At least a quarter of the choir left immediately and ran back as fast as they could down the way they had come. The new singer watched them go sympathetically, while the rest hesitated, in two minds whether to follow or to stay. Many were still pondering on this unknown Love of God.

'What kind of love is this?' they demanded, 'this love that allows terror and torture to innocent men and beasts?' There had been loving parents in some lucky lives, of course: a few loving friends, a loving teacher or two, loving cats and dogs. A few admitted that, not clearly knowing what love meant, they had recklessly given it to all sorts of undeserving persons, and been let down, dropped, deserted, and swiftly passed over or replaced. So did this God-love have infinite meanings then – all different from anything known on earth? If so, what was the use of talking about it?

'Time to talk or sing if we ever get to heaven!' came a shout. 'Right now, let's keep our mouths shut!'

There was complete silence, so much so that the old choirmaster came back to see what had happened. 'Are you working them up about something?' he asked the new member. 'If so I'll have to ask you to leave at once. I've put a life's work into training them, and I can't afford to hear it all go for nothing. What's more, I'm afraid I've changed my mind about the love-singing and even the love-talk. I'm into *Justice* now. *Justice* is the greatest thing on earth!'

'But will you let me stay and sing with your choir a little longer?' the young man asked.

'That's fair enough, of course. And I will stand and listen as hard as I can,' said Sam, stepping from the fringe of the forest into the sunlight.

The sound he heard was like light itself – sometimes flashing up through the trees and descending again into blackness through thick leaves, and once more climbing up a scale of brilliance till it reached a sunburst of sound. Bells, flutes and cymbals like those that herald the appearance of a new king were heard, and then a second descent into the dark evening shadow moving swiftly along the ground.

'Have they fallen on their knees to pray and praise then?' Sam asked incredulously, peering at the men and women on the ground.

'Not yet,' said the new singer. 'How on earth could they sing with tongues parched dry with thirst, with stomachs blown tight as drums with hunger?'

'But have they sung up forgiveness to God yet?' the old man asked.

'No, no,' the other answered again. 'He will not be forgiven for a long, long time. Only when the desert is green as an orchard, when the dying children get their milk and lose the look of wizened age. Only then.'

The old choirmaster stepped forward defiantly. 'Of course the *singing* sounded good,' he said. 'But I'm not sure what you're trying to do. Are you trying to be different from all other singers?'

'Yes, I suppose I am,' the other conceded.

'Then what exactly are you aiming at?' the old choirmaster went on. He had known all along that this particular singer was proud, if not actually arrogant. He had met all types in his profession – the cringing and the confident, loud-voiced braggarts and soft-voiced hypocrites, bullying voices and begging ones. Yet it was difficult to know where this particular voice fitted in. All he could vouch for was that it was a totally new and beautiful one. And so powerful it was that the man was automatically taken as leader.

The young man was silent for a while before answering Sam's question. 'You ask what I'm aiming at. I am helping people to forgive the Almighty One for all the terrible things He has allowed on earth – the unbelievable wretchedness and frightful pain. He has forgiven them for many things. Now they can forgive Him. *He* can never be human. *They* can never be gods, but at least they can show they are human and be proud of it.'

'Don't try to change my singers,' said the old choirmaster. 'It has taken me long enough to prevent the bending knee and that horrible, begging note.'

'There'll be none of that if I have anything to do with it,' the new member assured him. 'They must go on shouting and cursing for as long as they wish. First the God must be shown fearlessly all they have endured. Then He might be forgiven. You will let me stay a short time with your singers, then?'

Again the old choirmaster could only agree. He waited, rather jealously, to hear what other sound this newcomer would bring from his choir. The old man believed that he had heard all sounds produced by animal and human throat. But this was something else. Fearful sounds and words evoking frightful images; young men, women and children of every race sliced to the bone by guns, beheaded by bombs; the frightened breath of children waiting for doors to open in the night; the roar of the wounded lion, the scream of the trapped hare, the terrified bellow of beasts with rolling eyes, slung up for slaughter; the rumbling of earthquakes spurting from unknown depths. These were not sounds only from throat or ground. These were the sounds of Hell on earth.

The young leader lifted up his arms, urging the choir to louder and louder shouts of outrage. Then he raised his hand for silence. 'That was excellent!' he called. 'You have shown a magnificent fury for the things allowed by God. Now you can show forgiveness to match!'

Again the air was filled with furious mutterings and cries of complaint.

'You see, they are not stupid,' the old choirmaster explained. 'Most of the things we heard are the fault of Man. They have nothing to do with God. Anyway, He is above thanks or blame. To think anything else would be blasphemy.'

Old Sam had once hoped to be a popular preacher in a large city church with a decent stipend and a gathering of well-dressed ladies and gentlemen who would listen to him with unquestioning respect. How he longed, after all these years in the wilderness, to arrive at a cool, Christian building where there was no cursing, no obscenity, no endless questions and no striving on his part to offer quickfire explanations for every single horror that had ever happened upon earth!

He sidetracked a good deal of the argument nowadays. Yet he was still left with the humiliating desire to keep on with his own nagging questions, whether directed to an angel or devil in his own mind or even to some interloper who might happen, in passing, to step out of a dark wood. He turned again to the young singer for reassurance. 'It *is* the fault of human beings, isn't it?' he asked anxiously. 'The old barbaric gods would have allowed these horrors, of course, but not the great, good God of Love we have prayed and sung to day after day, year in year out.'

'I can promise great changes will come one day,' the younger man replied.

'One day, one year, one eternity,' added the old choirmaster, shaking his head dolefully.

The young man smiled. He had always foreseen more doubt than hope. One had to wait aeons and aeons of time for hope. Suddenly he left the path. He entered the forest again. Black darkness hid him.

'Is that young man gone for good?' asked one of the singers. 'I liked him. His standards were far too high, of course. He will never be popular.'

'He may well come again,' the choirmaster replied. 'He was simply here to see the damage and the pain for himself.'

'But who brought it on us?' the singer asked again.

'No doubt we brought it on ourselves,' said the old man.

'That is an easy answer,' said the other.

'Yes, I believe you're right,' the choirmaster agreed. 'It would take some superhuman power to bring all the catastrophe that has occurred on earth.'

'So that is the only answer you can find?'

'Well, I am only human,' said the old man. 'And I am tired. What more can I say? For the whole of my life I have been dumbfounded.'

Hearing this, the rest of the choir circled protectively around him. They were no longer angry. Doubt was more lovable than an iron faith, they decided. This looser circle they had formed let in both light and shadow. People felt free to break away from it and to come back again, to stand still, argue or be silent, to sing in tune or discord, to listen or to stop their ears. It was no sacred circle. Those who left were not followed or persuaded by love, the binding ties of friendship or the community spirit — to come back.

Over the centuries came changing groups of singers with their choirmasters. Rules changed. Tunes changed. Hopes rose and fell. Only music itself remained and the great forest of ancient trees. But every choirmaster taught his group not only how to sing, but to listen intently and to count the beat. Sometimes the songs were strident with bitterness, sometimes mellow with hope. Often for endless time there was no singing at all in the forest. But always an ardent listening for the return of a young leader hacking down branches to let in light — and for the terrible and confident crackle of His approaching footsteps over aeon upon aeon of fallen twigs.

Through the Forest

He lived on the outskirts of a huge, ancient forest, but as he grew older Martin began to be disenchanted with his walks there. That was the difficulty with fairy tales and why, he supposed, some parents and teachers advocated more down-to-earth reading for children. The forest tales had told of entering the great woods and remaining for years or perhaps for ever. After walking for ten miles or so an ugly but exceedingly wise dwarf would disclose the secret and the strangeness of one's birth and upbringing. Some years later and many miles further on one would meet the beautiful and ideal companion for life. Great happiness began and that was the end of it.

But there was something missing in the forest these days and something menacing. It was not in the fear of meeting wild animals. Most of the animals, wild or tame, had been shot. It was not in fear of darkness, because the gaps between the trees had become wider and wider in recent months and soon there was so much daylight to be seen that there was no possibility of losing oneself.

The fairy stories quickly faded in the light of day. In fact, as time went on, they began to seem foolish. Where were the lonely cottages where some old woman would emerge with bowls of soup for the cold and hungry? Where were the kindly old woodchoppers who pointed the way home to lost travellers? Often he felt a spurt of anger towards his parents who had brought him up on such tales when all the time they had known the true, hard facts and had hidden them from him.

However, one day – not far from the path – he did come on a cottage and, glancing through the window, saw a room full of people. Three or four girls caught sight of him and came out, led by a young woman in clean, blue dungarees. Her chest was firmly flattened by a clipboard from which hung a Biro on a chain. She looked him over through horn-rimmed spectacles. 'Did you bring anything to eat?' she asked. Martin looked puzzled. 'Anything to *eat*?' she repeated briskly. 'If you're joining us even for a day I'm afraid you have to bring your own food. We'll probably be here till evening.' She held out her board for him to inspect. 'As you know, we're collecting names,' she said, pointing to three columns already filled. 'We're fairly near the road here, so we get people coming from the city and also coming through the forest from the other side. We want to be completely unbiased ourselves, of course, though obviously we do know where we stand.' To Martin she looked exceedingly tough and biased, but as yet he didn't know on what side. He was intrigued. For a moment the old fairy tales came back – the good spells and the bad. Name collecting, name speaking could be a matter of witchcraft just as surely as the taking of photos, the painting of portraits could be to primitive tribes. Certainly this brisk young woman was not his idea of a witch, but his parents had misled him on so many things. They could have misled him on this one too.

The young woman held the board steady. 'If you could simply sign your name here,' she said, pointing to a clear space and handing him the pen on the chain.

'Just your full name and address, your age and phone number too, if you don't mind; and there's a space for anything else you might wish to say about yourself – married, single, divorced. Any brothers or sisters? Illnesses in the family. Your job, special interests, hobbies and that kind of thing. The name of your bank and your account number would be helpful. Are your parents still alive? Did you ask what we're here for?' She raised her head momentarily. 'We are speaking for the right of people to have houses built where they please, the right to have more and more freedom to spread, to build schools, churches, shops and offices with garages and transport nearby. Maybe a couple of cinemas, a dance-hall and a skating rink.'

'Did they tell you?' said Martin.

'Naturally, I don't know them myself personally. The city tells us what they want. The city speaks for all of us – for you, for me, for everyone. Perhaps you think you are alone in liking trees. As a matter of fact, I like trees as much as anyone else. But there's no use being romantic at the expense of others. Now they are making room for houses.'

'But there isn't room.'

'There's plenty of room!' She circled with her arm the sky, the ground, the leafy distances of trunk and twig. 'It's waste ground,' she said.

'No, it's a forest,' Martin replied, wishing that the leaves at least would rustle and snap in protest, that branches would sway and crack in violent gestures of grief and fury. But no wind sprang up to move them. They had no voice.

'You know I do believe you've got the wrong idea of me,' said the girl, smiling. 'Don't imagine I don't love nature.' The young man who was called Martin stared at her. She was a well-groomed girl. Her shoes were

very new – neither dirty nor down-at-heel. Her
fingernails were immaculate. Her face was calm and
well made up. Her hair would be trim and smooth until
the wind got at it. She had walked through sun and rain
without being torn or spat upon by pouncing trees,
without getting lost, being frightened by darkness,
startled by strange sounds, clawed by hateful thorns or
brought down by hidden roots. God knows she would
never be fool enough to eat the poison berries brought
by an evil witch. She had come by way of a superstore
and bought the morning-fresh sandwiches wrapped in
Clingfilm.

'It's just,' she explained, 'that people are more important than trees.' Martin glanced at the busy, unprepos-
sessing group behind her. There was no room for
sentimentality here. He saw at once that they were not
more important than trees. They might, at a pinch, be
more important than certain kinds of prickly bush. They
were undoubtedly more important than the over-
pruned trees on either side of a new thoroughfare, but
they did not appear, at this moment, half as important
as the great trees of the old forest. Nevertheless he
realised he was on dangerous territory. Might he not be
felled to the ground for such thoughts?

'Well, I see I've been mistaken,' said the girl, briskly
pressing her clipboard more firmly against her chest. 'I
see you are not *one of us*. Perhaps you'll come to a different, more human view when you've had time to think
about it. The trouble with you,' she said as a parting
shot, 'is that you're so immature. In fact, if you don't
mind me saying so, you're what we all call *green*.'

'Yes. Well, naturally I am. I've just joined it.'

'Joined what?'

'I've joined the Green Party.'

They stared at him pityingly. 'Fair enough,' said one,

'but it's got little to do with real day-to-day politics. Nothing to do with helping The People. Anyway we'll give you one or two forms to read, and you can contact us when you change your mind.' Martin noticed she said 'when' not 'if'. There were no 'ifs' amongst the pioneers of progress.

There was an assenting murmur amongst the group as they parted to let him through. Martin walked on. There was no wind and overhead there was silence. Under his feet it was quiet too with the silence of moss and herb, fed by centuries of sun and dew. Only the snap of a pine cone came to his ears and the sound of a bird tapping at snail shells in the leaves. He was a good deal shaken by the clipboard girl and by his own childish naïvety in thinking that any growing thing could now remain untouched. Again he was astounded that his careful guardians, teachers and elderly relations could have shown him endless pictures of flowers and green forests without pointing out the huge, smiling bill-boards on the outskirts, advertising toothpaste, cigarettes and Coca Cola. Why, in their stories of fairies, elves and angels had there been no warning of wild, screaming streets, the blocks of black factories, the smell and glitter of thousands of cars along the highway?

Now, as he walked on, he noticed that the path was gradually growing harder underfoot. The moss changed into smaller and smaller stones until he found himself walking along a newly gravelled path. Suddenly an electric saw started up in front of him, beginning as a thin whine and rising to a steady, skull-shattering scream. There were woodcutters here – not at all like the wood-choppers of his early stories, ever ready to tell a gormless traveller some unlikely tale of the woods. No, this lot were getting on with it as quickly as possible, ready to talk when the job on hand was finished. The sound

of the screaming saw stopped suddenly and total silence
beat about the spot. The men stood watching Martin
in amiable amusement. 'You've not heard that sound
before?' Martin shook his head.

'Where have you been living all this time then?'
Martin indicated vaguely some distant place on the other
side of the forest. He was loath to confess his ignorance
of what went on in any other part.

'Well give it a year or two or even less, and you're
going to see a few tidy rows of bungalows going up
along here and a broad main road, of course. We'll see
a beauty once the concrete's down, with lamps and all
to come. Obviously it's going to take longer than the
plan. Pedestrian crossings. Stop and Go. Ladies and
Gents. Bins. Shelters. Telephones. The lot. Nobody
knows where the money comes from or even who
wants the things. But they always come in the end, no
matter if the talk goes on for months.'

'But I never thought you'd gone so far already,' said
Martin. 'There's a crowd back amongst the trees who
are still collecting names.'

'There's always funny folk among the trees,' said the
woodman. 'What names?'

'People who agree and disagree. It's all been agreement as far as I can see.'

'Makes not a bit of difference,' said the other. 'The
whole thing's settled and done with long ago. Years and
years ago.' He gave a crack of laughter. 'Surely you
didn't think a huge job like this was going to wait for
agreement!' he exclaimed scornfully. The saws screamed
behind him and two great dinosaur cranes lowered their
necks, opened their jaws, gulped greedily at a hole in
the earth and creaked on. The workman looked sympathetically at the young man's face. 'Real brutes, aren't
they?' He stared at the wood-strewn ground. 'Don't

worry,' he said, 'all the bits of good wood round here won't be wasted. Most of the better stuff will be shifted to factories. They'll be used for making wooden spoons, toys, chests, tables and what have you. Some of the better chunks go to the monastery up there, so I've heard. I believe the monks like making wooden bowls. A good relaxing thing to do between prayers and keeps them out of mischief, I suppose. Though where the mischief comes from on that cold, windswept hill beats me, it really does. It must come from inside, mustn't it? Well, everyone's got their own ideas. But there's something about wood they go for, I believe. It's natural, you see. Good, clean and natural. But the funny thing about being natural too long – it begins to get *un*natural. Yes, all good people are supposed to like wood. The rest of us go for the flashy stuff – the brass, tin, steel and aluminium, and gold and silver, naturally, if you can get your hands on it. Well, I never meddle with things that aren't my line. Everyone's got their own ideas. Leave them to get on with it is what I say. I believe they get up in the middle of the night to pray. I couldn't do that myself though sometimes when I've been out with the boys I get up once or even twice, though certainly not to pray. Talking about being unnatural, you look a bit out of this world yourself. Where do you come from?'

'From the other side of the forest.'

'So you've never been properly out?'

'Oh yes. I had to, of course,' said Martin. 'I went off to school like everyone else. Then I came back.'

'No good,' said the other. 'Once you've got out, never go back. And you're still too young to be shocked at changes like the ones around here. Don't think I don't detest some things myself. But then I'm far too old to shout and kick about it.'

'I'm going to shout and kick all my life about ugly things,' said Martin. He added that his father had once taught woodwork in a small school on the far side of the city.

'There, you see!' exclaimed the woodman. 'Your father's a *good* man. He's a lover of wood like our friends the monks up there.'

'I don't believe he ever made bowls,' said Martin. 'He made a wheelbarrow once. Mostly it was chests he made. Tables and chests. Years ago he used to make bookcases. But it's all different now. You've got to make them for ornaments, not books – for crinolined ladies, fat cupids and what have you, standing on shallow shelves. Still, he always used good wood. He's old-fashioned of course, but I think he *is* a good man.' He stood for a moment looking into the half-sawed branches above them. Already the tallest tree was lying on the ground with the woodchips and sawdust on top of a tangled heap of shattered twigs and a frenzy of leaves.

'Now you'll be asking about birds,' said the woodman, following his eyes. 'They'll just have to find other places, won't they? Just like everything else, like the moths, the bats and butterflies, the hedgehogs, the hares and the foxes. I hope you're not the sort who thinks it helps to take one bird or bat home out of its misery, while driving your mother round the bend.'

'I'm not an idiot,' Martin replied.

'I never said so. I believe I'd join you if I could,' said the man, picking up a great barrow of red earth. 'Anyway, I'll see you around.'

Martin walked slowly back through the forest to his home. He said nothing to his parents of what he'd seen that day or whom he'd talked to. He didn't often cross the forest after that, and the days passed slowly as usual.

Occasionally he wrote a few mediocre verses. His father and mother were delighted. They said that nothing would please them better than that he should become a poet – a good or even a great one. Lots of other parents, they added, would hate this idea. But they would love it. From that moment he wrote no more verse.

Martin's father was now in his late sixties and he was glad enough to retire from teaching. It had taken a long time to reach the school by the roundabout bus that circled the forest. The new houses going up on the other side had meant that his classes had become larger and larger. As for his mother, she saw few people. She was becoming frail and rather querulous. She said that trees were her only friends, but it seemed that wood itself was not included. She complained of her husband's job. He brought in sawdust on his shoes and scattered wood-chips around the place. There were, of course, no shops near, but a few large vans were now moving about the place. Because of the growing housing schemes on the far side they carried everything that anyone could possibly wish for in a forest including romantic paperbacks, insect repellent, shoe polish, high-class writing paper and denture cream. Martin dropped all poetry and began to paint a little – studies of trees gesticulating against luminous puffball clouds. Again his parents were overjoyed. There had been painters as well as poets in the family. They took pains to buy him a box of the most expensive paints and a fistful of genuine horsehair brushes. His mother was just about to buy him a voluminous linen smock with pleats down the back and front when he said he had changed his mind. What did he want to do then? He wanted, at this moment, to do nothing. His mother, on the whole, was a patient person. It was her one great virtue, but she made the mistake of showing it day and night. Such patience made her son angry. Two winters later Martin's mother died of a dangerous flu, and bad conscience was added to his other feelings. The father now confessed to his son that he'd had a quiet but rather a disappointing life. He didn't enlarge on this, but Martin decided that, though his own life was quiet – quieter than that of any other young man he'd ever known – yet it must never end in patience and disappointment. His father was now over eighty and did not have long to live.

'If it will cheer you, father,' said Martin one day, 'I'd like you to know that I'm going to take up painting after all.' His father was overjoyed. 'Oh, if only your poor mother were alive to hear it. Your uncle Joe was a painter, and your second cousin – the one in America – *called* himself a painter, though, in my poor judgement, not a good one. Plates. Teapots and fruit. He tried to be a Cubist, but far too late. That was his mistake, of course. Square apples and grapes like those strange oblong green beads your mother wore. I suppose he was clever. He even managed to get indecency into his painting of pillows. Hard to believe, but there it was, art or no art. I'm afraid it was no art with him. But you – I know you've got the right stuff in you to make a painter!' There was silence for some moments.

'But I won't be painting *pictures*, father, so don't worry,' said Martin. 'I mean to be a housepainter. That's what I've wanted to be for years.'

Martin saw that this was another disappointment, but his father was used to these as he'd said, and his life was now short. He said nothing against his son's ambition – simply gave the whole idea his blessing and only asked that the young man should use only the very best brushes, pails and paints for his trade, that his planks and ladders should be safe and strong and that he should get the highest pay for the job. There had been quite a bit of money in the family, he said, and now it was all his. The father did not live long after this. Martin was surprised and pleased that, so soon after death, his face seemed to change. The expression of quiet patience and disappointment gradually sharpened into a look of strange, peering alertness and expectancy. His son wondered if this might indeed be the sight of heaven in the far distance between close-set trees.

Martin now tidied up the house ready to sell it. Most people who came into the forest passed it without interest. One day, however, a romantic, middle-aged widow came round to view it. She didn't care for the cramped, untidy house, but she took an immediate fancy to the young man. This alarmed him. He saw that it was the extraordinary convenience and economy of the arrangement that had struck her. A pleasant middle-aged bachelor living alone could be thrown in with some useful items of furniture – all going dirt cheap. She asked him if he was lonely. He replied that he was not. She asked him if he had always been a lover of trees and forests. He replied that he was now beginning to hope for other things in his life. He was careful not to specify what these things might be in case she would offer them on the spot. She asked what he was going to do now that he was quite alone. He said he was going to paint. The woman said it was one of the most romantic things she had ever heard – a man alone on the edge of a great forest who was setting out to be a great painter. He replied that his painting was probably not the sort she had in mind. When he had learnt the trade he was going to paint the interiors and exteriors of the houses on the other side of the forest. In fact, he intended to buy one himself and start from there.

Eventually Martin sold his house to a botanist and his wife. He took an immediate liking to them both. He noticed how, after a cursory examination of the place, they kept moving towards the windows and stayed there looking out for a long time. The wife made no mention of measuring the rooms at once for curtains or carpets, and her husband, though he mentioned the creakings and crackings of the place, took no steps to see if all the floorboards were sound. They seemed, in fact, more interested in the scene outside. There was still a great strip of trees beyond the house, but Martin warned them that the scene would soon look very different. Many more houses would certainly go up on the other side. The strips of sunlight between the trees they were looking at now would eventually be cut by paths and even busy roads. They might be staring at an illusion, he added. One day the forest would not exist.

'Well, isn't everything an illusion?' said the botanist. 'We're looking down, up and sideways into a universe that doesn't exist in any way we can possibly conceive. But at least we can remember and enjoy the illusion. I'd remember these trees, for instance, even if they disappeared tomorrow – even if they turned overnight into masts and telegraph poles.' He added that long ago he'd given up the idea of anything in heaven or earth being lasting. The whole thing was totally mysterious, a mind-blowing process of metamorphosis.

This was a great relief and comfort to Martin. It was as if he could hand over to these benevolent strangers everything that the forest meant to him – the blessing and burden of ancient trees, their strength and fragility in the modern world, the tragedy of their disappearance, and even the unexpected friendliness of those who had put axe and saw to them. Now all these emotions could be left to the incomers. As a duty he mentioned all the things that could be made with the spare wood – cooking spoons, breadboards, stools, toys, bookends, trays and boxes. 'I daresay there will soon be a shop over on the other side that would take and sell all of them,' he added.

'We're not really interested in what can be made from bits of wood,' said the woman. 'My husband simply likes to study trees and everything that grows under them. I'm writing a book myself. This place is ideal for that.' She mentioned fairy tales.

'I never cared for those,' said Martin cautiously. 'I heard them all as a child. Rather cruel and sad they seemed. Nobody ever met the kind and beautiful people passing by in the distance.'

In a few weeks he had moved out. But the clearing of the house had taken him a long time. He discovered that his parents had been more interesting and even more secretive people than he'd imagined. His mother had kept old letters in a shoe box – letters from some young man written to her when she was a girl. They were unusually personal letters, expressing thoughts and feelings, but never mentioning love. Obviously for her, however, their long sojourn inside a box and hidden, like bulbs, in a dark cupboard, had turned them into love letters – precious things ready for a future flowering that had not materialised. His father had collected only things connected with his work – the tools of his wood-work days along with the designs for things that had never been made. There were also a few bowls that had not come up to the mark and had been scrapped. Either they had not been perfectly round or there was some almost invisible flaw on their surface. Along with these there was one photo of his father. This photo – very spry, very bright-eyed and hopeful – made Martin feel sad. He had only seen a different side. So was there no way the young were ever going to know their hidden parents except as tired and rather desperate people, long past their best, if there had ever been a best?

One day he abruptly stopped his search into the past. He swept up the place one last time, then sat down and waited for the van that was to take him and his possessions to his new bungalow on the other side. He never turned his head as it drove off and his cottage disappeared like a small ship going down in a green sea.

It was some time before he got to work on his next place, but meanwhile he put up a prominent sign inviting orders for painting and decorating the neighbouring houses. Their owners were not slow to answer. There had been many changeovers even in the last ten years or so. Martin soon found himself inside rooms where, before painting, he would have to strip and scrape down into the recent past like an archaeologist of wallpaper. He found himself uncovering bizarre ambitions and longings. Carefully and tenderly he peeled away old fears and desires. Sometimes someone's longing to get away was suddenly revealed by a paper covered with ships, aeroplanes and sleek motorcars. Certain kitchens and dining rooms boasted old wallpapers covered with wine bottles and glasses, tropical fruits hanging in branches, and crisscrossing designs of knives, forks and spoons. Nurseries had wallpapers of bears and dolls, drums and pink bows overlaid by other designs as the children grew older. In some bedrooms he stripped off naked dancing girls with pumpkin breasts. Occasionally he came on a tree paper vainly trying to echo the vanishing forest. He uncovered clouds, stars, moons and flowers. Soon he began to repaper every room. Before long he was ready to paint the outside of certain houses – their doors, windows, railings and garages. He offered a restricted choice of colours to his clients. He told them he used only soft shades of green and blue. He also used purple, brown and black. 'These are the forest colours,' he would say to all objections and queries.

'But the forest will soon not exist,' the bungalow people insisted. 'And these are houses, not trees. We can't go back to the monkey stage, can we?' They had lived a long time beside a dark forest, they said, and now they wanted to take bright yellow to the doors, to outline the railings in brilliant scarlet.

'Do you want your great-grandchildren to remember you when they dig up ugly planks of shiny yellow, when they trip over lethal splinters of scarlet railing?' said Martin.

'Anyway, nothing matters now,' said the old pessimist of the district, 'whether our houses are red, yellow or black. Soon concrete will cover everything. Concrete's the strongest stuff in the world,' he added as he watched a huge machine rolling out the stuff in the distance.

'Don't you believe it!' exclaimed Martin. 'Living trees are stronger than dead concrete, stronger even than all the lifeless metal in the world. Tree roots can pass through cracks as thin as threads. They can burst through steel vaults. No. You'll never get rid of the trees. Never.'

'We'll see,' said the neighbour. 'Meanwhile we'd better stop theorising and get on with the painting. I'm not too keen on nature talk. It begins sensibly enough, but ends with cranks knocking their heads together.'

'By the way,' Martin remarked after a while, 'are the monks still around? It was said they were keen on wood. Wooden bowls, to be exact.'

'Begging bowls, you mean?' the other asked suspiciously.

'No, just plain, round wooden bowls. You can get them from the craft shop down there. Natural circles, you understand. Something to do with perfection. It all appeals to the religious outlook, I daresay.'

'Oh, I don't know about that,' said the householder. 'My wife's got a thing about bowls too. Bowls on every shelf and table, in every corner. Wooden, china, metal, glass – you name it. She collects them wherever she goes. And I can tell you straight off it's nothing to do with perfection. She's very far from perfect as she'd be the first to admit. I wouldn't know about the monks, of course, but I *do* happen to know my own wife.'

The road was becoming more used to Martin's forest colours by the time he came to paint the outside of the bungalows. Even from an aeroplane the houses, on the edge of ground where trees had once grown, looked more at home. They now appeared to grow out of the landscape instead of being stuck on like separate, bright bricks. The saws still screamed amongst the few trees left. The concrete was gradually going down and in some months the road might be ready for heavy traffic. But Martin was thought of as some sort of mediator between city and forest. His large brushes stroked the walls, gates, railings of houses steadily, confidently. Yet people would still stand round to watch and question: 'Why do you use that dark blue?'

'I'm bringing the evening sky down into it,' he would reply. 'I'm trying to bring back those deep forest pools that have all dried up.'

'Is that not too dark a brown, Martin?' they would say, pointing to certain parts of the outside woodwork.

'Well, it's not as dark as the earth after that great thunderstorm, if you remember,' he would say.

'And what about that green on the garages? That could be more cheerful, couldn't it? It's a real gloomy green.'

'Yes. Late summer is always dark in the forest.'

Once in a while Martin would cross over to visit the botanist and his wife. They now looked out on to a very different scene. The new road across the ancient forest was coming nearer. They knew the sound of saws, of crashing trees, and finally the noise of traffic would one day burst through.

'I never knew it would be as bad as that when I sold the place,' said Martin.

'Well, how could you?' said the botanist's wife. 'It was up to us to find out.'

'The first idea was to leave a wide strip of forest on this side,' Martin went on. 'I saw the plans, in fact.'

'Plans go for nothing when money comes into it,' she said. 'We saw plans too. A very nice man pointed it all out on the map. Of course I see now he thought we were a pair of dear old sentimental things who'd be happy with a flower patch and a garden gnome. He told us he loved trees himself. It really seemed as if he couldn't bear to see a twig fall off, let alone a tree lying on the ground. When we saw him off he murmured: "Life must go on, you know." But we've enjoyed living here and we'll stay as long as we can. I'm still writing a book, but I'm finished with fairies and forests. It'll have to be water now. We've always been travellers so we'll move off while we can to some great lake or river. My husband's an expert on water plants too, so that will suit him. Surely nothing will happen to dry up the water unless it's a nuclear disaster.'

'Will you be moving away soon?' Martin asked.

'No, luckily they're not going to knock us down just yet. They're just going to surround us with new houses. And we're to be "landscaped" to keep us quiet. A few trees and bushes and a patch of grass, I suppose. When the road reaches us we'll move to some lake or other as I've told you. Meantime I'm going to start up a small woodland tearoom or something of the kind. I've no conscience, I'm afraid. We need a lot of money if we're to move away, and I can make it. The tearoom will try its best to be twee, olde-worlde and horrible, but I hope to nip that in the bud. The place will become more and more expensive, even fashionable. People will drive out from the city and from all the new housing estates, and I shall slave for hours. I shall make an unusual jam from berries. It will be called Forest Conserve. Conserve, not jam, because we can give talks on conservation at the same time and encourage discussion. My husband obviously knows the eatable from the poisonous berries, so that should be all right. I shall have to learn to cook and bake at last, and he can talk about plants and trees till the cows come home. The tearoom will probably be called "The Botanist's Bothy". It will be very exclusive and will be a tremendous draw even to those who have hardly seen a leaf.'

'I've never met such an optimist!' Martin exclaimed.

'I might as well be. Jack is the pessimist. The mixture's explosive, stimulating, or whatever word you want to call it. At any rate, we're too old for marriage guidance. Years and years ago we went, but I fell madly for one of the guiders and botched the whole thing up. But to go back to jam. Eventually this special conserve of mine may reach the city shops. The jars should bear a special tree label designed by a proper artist. You *are* an artist, aren't you?'

'No, I'm told I'm not – not the kind you're talking about. I paint houses, doors, walls and windows. I'm a housepainter. By the way, I expect you'll be needing lots of wooden plates and bowls for your Bothy. Probably chairs, stools and tables too. You can get them all from the craft shop on the other side.'

'I'm not a crafty person, as a matter of fact,' said the

botanist's wife. 'Are you trying to bring us all together? I'll look over sometime, of course.'

'Then there are the monks up there,' Martin went on. 'When you've made enough, why don't you try some of your jam with them? Everything good and natural would be welcome there.'

'I haven't even made the stuff yet, and I very much doubt if I'm good and natural myself,' she replied. 'But I'll think it over.'

A year or so later, climbing down from the window of a house where he'd been painting, Martin caught a glimpse of pale green on the path below. He bent down and saw a single seedling pushing up between the flag-stones. This excited him like the sudden sight of a new comet to an astronomer, or like the feathers and leaves blown towards an early ship of discovery – signs that some huge, unknown continent was near. He didn't dare touch the fragile green thing, but was across within the hour to his friend, the botanist. Quickly they came back together to study every detail of this new life – its straight, determined stem and the infinitesimal green leaves.

'Yes, there you've got it!' exclaimed the botanist, rising triumphantly and dusting his knees. 'Your first oak tree and, if you're lucky, the beginning of a forest!'

'You mean if we live for four or five hundred years?'

'Well then, let your heirs and all their distant offspring have it. In no time the trees will be strong. They'll push down the houses, topple the poles and cover the concrete. In some hundreds of years' time people may have learned something. Stupidity can't go on forever. They may long for wood rather than iron, for strong roots to strangle the steel. Have you *seen* the roots of trees? Ferocious, tenacious, and so strong centuries of gales won't move them.'

'Yet this seedling could be crushed in seconds,' said Martin.

'Of course,' replied the botanist, 'but jungles have covered civilisations with a green so powerful you could hardly drag it off the stone.'

'But you can't stop progress on the earth,' said Martin.

'What progress?' asked the botanist.

'New machines, new rockets, new satellites, new robots, new bombs, new space-probes to the great Computer God in the sky. I only paint houses but I've tried to paint in forest colours. But do people *want* green? No, they want yellow, scarlet, electric-blue, orange and pink inside and out. Green's supposed to be unlucky and always has been. Ask your wife. Ask in any shop. Who wants to wear green?'

'Well, I don't know anything about superstition,' said the botanist. 'I just know the earth always wants to wear green and always has done. Leave it alone for a few years and look again. Everything has gradually disappeared except green. What's lucky for the earth can't be unlucky for people, can it?'

They now hurried back to fetch the botanist's wife who agreed that green was supposed to be unlucky, but in nothing else she could think of but clothes. She herself, however, donned an apple-green skirt to show she was no party to superstition. She accompanied the men to the gardens at the other side of the forest to look at the seedling. Quite a few neighbours from adjoining gardens now gathered when they saw two men and a woman staring fixedly at the crack between the paving stones. Most stayed away, suspecting something horrible. One man, in fact, shouted across his fence: 'Is it a *snake*?'

'There, you see,' said the housepainter. 'People expect

a *snake* in the grass, never the grass itself. Very soon they'll see only snakes and no grass. Can you blame them?'

Nevertheless, when the people of the road discovered what the three were staring at they searched their own paths and gardens. Suddenly there were shouts from one side and the other or even from upper windows where people were looking down. Yet they were peculiarly mixed shouts – mostly shadowy and doubtful, yet gradually lit here and there with a glimmer of hope. It seemed as if those who'd lived on the edge of great trees at first could hardly recognise a green seedling. But soon more and more people were looking for them. They went running here and there into one another's gardens, bumping together in their search as if enacting a clumsy fallback into Eden – that magnificent memory of green trees. Soon there would be no more discussion about forest colours in a house. It was the forest itself they longed for. Naturally there were those who mocked at the fuss over this colour green. Weren't lots of awkward things green? Mould was green. Phlegm was green. And so was immaturity. Above all they laughed at the idea of green ever covering the engines of destruction. How could greenness ever get a grip on the smooth, round bombs, or take root on the slippery satellites of war? But the botanist himself knew how childish the idea of greenness could become if it meant only grass and plants covering the surface of the earth like a comfortable, plushy carpet. He spoke up now about the destruction – as weapons and poison took over – of all fruits and crops, the disappearance of all peoples and animals, the poisoning of air, sea and soil to unknown, enormous depths. He stopped all talk of seedlings. Instead he lectured them on science. 'What will the earth become if we carry on as we've been doing?' he asked at the end of his talk one night. There was silence and he answered himself: 'A small, stinking poisoned pill in space.' A few successful businessmen who'd continually and comfortably travelled the earth took affront at the name 'poisoned pill'. They asked the botanist to illustrate his ideas to an audience. He complied and showed them great parts of the sky on screen. It was just possible – though not very likely – that man was unique, he said, while pointing to swirling blue veils of nebulae, infinitely distant in time and space.

But the botanist's lifespan was not infinite. The old man caught a chill one evening as he sat outside his cottage and not many weeks later he died. He was buried on the far side of the forest where, months afterwards, it was observed that many small, green seedlings were growing up around the mound of his grave. Though no doubt the seeds had come on the wind, others assumed they had been carefully planted by the gardeners of the road. Up at the monastery it was put down without question as a true miracle of God. Whichever way it was, he lay – after many years had passed – in a grove of tall, green trees.

The botanist's wife lived on alone, keeping her house and tearoom going at the edge of the forest. The visitors to the tearoom increased and even her jam, Forest Conserve, was beginning to make its name in distant city stores. She made an arrangement with the craft shop at the other side which still took wood from the forest to make small tables, bowls, stools and wooden spoons. The botanist's wife helped to advertise all these at her own tables and got a substantial cut of the gains. Every summer she took several pots of her jam up to the monks. Luckily, the head of the monastery loved Forest Conserve. It was an indulgence which at first he had only grudgingly allowed himself. Now, as he grew

older, he positively craved it. Often they chatted
together and on one visit she enquired if he would care
for some beautiful, hand-turned wooden bowls as well
as jam. She went on to ask discreetly about the unbroken
circle as a sign of perfection. Shortly afterwards the
monastery acquired a set of bowls at bargain price, and
the shop with its holy back-up became known far and
wide. Again the botanist's widow made a good thing
out of it and at the same time was praised by the head
of the order for bringing a steady stream of sweetness
on to the long tables of the refectory. They had many
talks together on religion, on love, death, heaven and
hell, good and evil. She congratulated him warmly on
the curious fact that he – a confirmed bachelor living in
a wood without apple trees or women – should have
such a deep and detailed knowledge of the sin of Eve,
and advised him that the average woman like herself
had little time or opportunity for the more interesting
sins. Over the years they became close friends.

The housepainter lived on, but as he grew older he
was a little more careful about climbing ladders.
Though he was in and out of many houses he was still
an outsider and a lonely man. He was not so fussy now
about his colours, though still drawing the line at scarlet
and shocking pink for doors and windows. Often as he
painted he sang and whistled like a bird in a high tree.
He rejoiced that after some hundreds of years no roof
that he had painted, no window, wall or chimney pot
would be seen for green.

The Stroke

𝔐 Mr William Sibald, a city banker, sat beside the phone in the hospital corridor almost on the point of tears. He was not ashamed of this. Long ago he had got over shame. Indeed he was relieved that all the things that were supposed to divide the sexes now seemed far behind in the rigidly controlled world he had left only two weeks before. Expressions of fear or downright terror, the open show of love, anguish, anxiety and grief could be expressed in here without apology. But like the warm and cold spots of the body there were certain areas of the hospital particularly susceptible to emotion. The phone area was one of these. For it was the place linking one to home and friends. Here men and women sat openly laughing and crying and sometimes breaking into angry words.

The routine followed a familiar pattern. The patient, while still in the ward, would prepare himself for long enough to phone husband or wife, son, daughter or friend. He would think up the message which, as time was limited, had to include the pressing in of money, the warmth of a greeting plus an absolute clarity in delivering the important words. All these had to come together at the right moment. Very often the message concerned something missing or more likely irretrievably lost.

For like all his fellow-patients Mr Sibald searched

constantly, and with increasing anxiety for his belong-
ings – his money, his paper, his spectacles, the slyly
slipping belt of his dressing-gown, his comb, his diary,
his address book, his pen and his watch. It was no different from the women in the next ward who dived constantly into huge handbags, zipping and unzipping
dozens of flaps and pockets, searching for their lost
selves – a scattered identity closely bound up with the
same pens and purses, lists and letters as the men, but
with the extra anxiety of safety pins and brooches,
hairslides and scissors, compacts, photos, lipsticks and
nailfiles. They searched for all these, but sometimes,
more despairingly, for the handbag itself which time
and time again would be retrieved from under the bed
or behind the locker by doctors, nurses, cleaners, or
maybe by the plumber who came to examine the pipes,
and above all by the newspaper boy who acted not only
as messenger from the outside world, delivering its
horrors and pleasures, but also, more importantly, as
the sharp-eyed finder of all things lost in the enclosed
world of hospital wards where, morning and evening,
he was watched by scores of anxious eyes as he ducked
and flitted from bed to bed. This time it was the banker's
watch that had been lost for a day and a night.

Here, amongst patients, William Sibald was reason-
ably patient: but on the whole he was an impatient man.
As manager of his bank, he was certainly impatient of
any slackness on the part of those who worked under
him. But latterly, in the evenings, on doctor's advice,
he had tensed himself to do nothing at all. The strain
had proved too much. Tonight, even in here, his
impatience had surged up. Earlier that evening he had
watched the mobile phone being wheeled round the
ward. It had stopped at an irascible old man who was
telling his daughter-in-law in no uncertain terms, and

with blistering asides for nearby nurses, that he was to be called for next day and at the earliest possible hour of that day. Mr Sibald, whose sympathy with the outside world was not just now at its strongest, yet had a flashing feeling for this woman somewhere at the other end of the line. He imagined her pale and horrified at what she heard – perhaps already about to make up his bed or stuffing his warm clothes into a bag ready for an early return journey across town.

That night, then, the banker had decided on the more private phone further up the corridor, and by some miracle had found his purse and extracted two ten-pence pieces. He then climbed laboriously out of his bed and into his gaping red slippers. He thought of these slippers as by far the friendliest of his clothes. They struck him as unbelievably patient objects which would wait endlessly, comfortably, until he was strong enough to get out of bed and walk, unaided. They seldom got lost, but remained in the same place at the side of his bed. There was no struggle to put them on. They had no laces, buckles, hooks or fasteners like some footwear, and they were visible to him at all times of the day and night – visible but not ostentatious, unlike the scarlet dressing-gown with silk lapels and tasselled belt his wife had bought him shortly after his illness. It was difficult to imagine what kind of illness could live up to such a flamboyant garb. Certainly a wounded crusader might have been proud to wear it, or some swaggering sea captain struck down by a freak wave on the deck.

There was nothing of the crusader or captain about Mr Sibald. At an unusually early age and in the midst of life he had suffered a slight stroke and was unable to hold his head as high as he would like. He had also suffered an impairment of one hand which, for a time, had made him doubt if he would ever be able to deal with his papers again, far less riffle through a wad of banknotes. However, this particular evening after supper he had collected himself and his coins together, had got himself out into the corridor and into the chair beside the phone where he waited – the phone being engaged. This evening, there were still a good many people about – doctors making a late visit, auxiliaries loaded with bundles of linen, the drugs sister with the rattling trolley of pills and bottles, and even the odd therapist still searching for her reluctant patient.

Once or twice the kitchen door opposite him would be half-opened on to a sudden glimpse of hot-faced women wiping dry huge, metal pans or arranging dish-towels on a low pulley. These were the patients from therapy who had been persuaded to practise kitchen skills before going home to 'normal' life. Some around here looked abnormally impatient patients, capable once more of clashing down pot lids, of snatching dusters off the rope, of thumping the iron down furiously upon damp dishcloths. Others could be glimpsed under the watchful eye of the cook – stirring, chopping, awkwardly peeling – like marionettes returned to fretful life.

Amongst older men in the corridor he was amazed to see two youths go by, stiff and pale, with unbelieving eyes. Yet other youngish men went past, far worse afflicted than himself – some with heads drooping, some with an arm across their chests as if defending themselves against a second quaking of the earth.

Behind them all came a woman in a magnificent white, quilted dressing-gown and white, fur-trimmed slippers, carrying two large vases of long-stemmed pink carnations. He watched her go into a side cupboard near the kitchen where she started to rearrange the vases beside the sink, refilling them under the tap and taking out withered blooms. There was a mirror above the

sink and once or twice she stopped what she was doing
to arrange her hair. The banker thought of her as some
handsome and successful hostess preparing for her
dinner guests. He imagined very clearly the woman and
her husband in their beautiful, cold, lonely Edinburgh
dining room. He knew these rooms very well. They
were the magnificently formal rooms where, on first
entering, guests didn't at once look to one another, but
instead looked about them, commenting for a long time
on the elegance of the marble mantelpiece or of the high,
white ceiling with its intricate cornice of grapes and
pomegranates, its icy scrolls, shells, ivies, rosettes and
vine leaves. Then there was the fantastic length of the
white windows outlined against the night. At these
windows first-time guests felt silenced, as though swept
away down precipitous drops of stone to a dark river
or round the curve of the classic crescent past lit, empty
windows. And somewhere, far out, lay the black sea
pinpointed with the lights of trawlers going north.

It was the combination of wild and formal in this city.
These heavy thuds and batterings on a windy night, in
contrast to the absolute calm within; these gulls and
scraps of paper rising in the air in contrast to the tidy
drawing room; all gave new guests an eerie sensation.
Who were these hosts and hostesses who turned not a
hair while birds and scraps rose to their sills, who could
converse politely while staring out calmly to the stormy
pavement and garden below? The visitors would, of
course, eventually discover one another and begin talking. Nevertheless, the more awkward might remain for
part of the evening gazing hopefully at some winged
head supporting a marble archway, waiting for the lips
to open and draw them into conversation, or waiting,
perhaps, for the wind to scream through cracks or

keyholes and throw them forcibly together. They cannot do it for themselves.

The bank manager had never suffered in this way. In his work – though he had seen many anxious, even suicidal people – he made few personal contacts. He had certainly never expected to be loved by his fellow-men, far less chatted up by angel lips. Indeed, he had been brought up to believe there was a good deal of strength to be gained, some disappointment avoided, by not expecting much affection from either man or woman.

By now the woman in the quilted dressing-gown had finished her flower arrangement in the cupboard and appeared again, triumphantly carrying her vases back to her ward. Still more patients passed him, making for the TV lounge – each enclosed in his own world, some with sure, swinging gait, measuring their steps, glassy eyes fixed on an unmoving goal. These were the ones who had been taught to walk again over the weeks. Fearfully, yet proudly, they glided past like mysterious ballet dancers newly risen from some catastrophic fall that might or might not bring their careers to nothing at one blow. One or two had given up the struggle and were leaning on the wall as against the side of a tilting ship.

The phone was still engaged. A powerful-looking old woman had been standing giving instructions to her daughter at home – lists of things to be brought in, reminders about the running of the house in her absence, orders on who was and who was not to come and visit her in hospital, questions about the safety of her jewellery, her bank-books, her letters, her money. Again the banker gained a brief vision of things at the other end of the line. He had seen the daughter during visiting hours as she passed the open door of the men's ward and went, laden, into the adjoining one to see her mother.

Occasionally she would appear in the lounge with the tall, complaining old woman on her arm. As far as he could see, no affectionate look ever passed from mother to daughter. Mr Sibald wondered if any praise or sympathy for the younger woman could ever seem sufficient now. He decided it could not. The exhausted-looking daughter in her fifties had no doubt often been commended for looking after the difficult old woman. But she would never marry now or have children. She would see nothing of the world and hardly anything of old friends. For the first time it occurred to the banker that friends had to be made. They did not arrive, smiling, on the doorstep of some tied-down man or woman. When her mother died the daughter, on the advice of relatives, might turn her mother into some kind of saint. The chances were she would feel guilty for small things left undone, for the passing bitter thought, for some unworthy dream in the night of freedom. The banker – not an imaginative man – was surprised how clearly he could visualise the elderly daughter at the end of the phone. Often he'd met her speaking gently, coaxingly to her mother along the corridors and in the visiting lounge. Was she herself a saint? Again he decided no. She wasn't tough enough, and saints were very tough, sometimes ruthless beings, well able to stand up for themselves, through thick and thin. They were adventurers, explorers, leaders, for the most part. Few of them had sat at home with families, looking after young or old. Suddenly the commanding voice of the old woman stopped. The phone was free at last.

And now Mr Sibald moved into the free place and put in his coin. The heart-rending failures at the phone very often happened just after the first coin had been pressed into the slot and after the familiar voice had come through. This, in itself, was moving enough for most people and was the reason why they were so slow to answer and why panic overtook them as, after a while, a mechanical buzz replaced the voice. It was this last difficulty that overwhelmed the banker. This man who had handled money all his life, had found himself unable to press another coin into the metal slot. For a while his wife's 'hallos' had gone on, loudly at first and then more softly, like some spurned woman determined to keep up a hopeful greeting to some man who'd sworn never to answer again in life. When the last 'hallo' died out and the buzz had started he banged down another coin with his fist, first angrily, then despairingly. 'Are they *all* bent, *all* damaged?' he cried, extending his outrage to the whole hospital and every limping patient moving past. He had now dropped the last coin he possessed on the floor. He searched hopelessly in his empty purse.

He was not left long in this predicament. From the open door of the kitchen a group of nurses surrounded him like a crowd of white, stiff-winged birds in defence of a fledgling that has come to grief. There was a flurry as four girls bent to search the floor, and a voice cried: 'Here it is!' A fearful tiredness came over the man before he could turn to the phone again. 'It's all right. Don't worry,' cried another. 'Give me the number and the message. And then don't worry. Just get back to bed.' The manager was helped back to the ward, a nurse at either elbow and a third gently pressing his back. As though from a long distance behind him he heard the voice speaking to his wife. 'A message from Mr Sibald. Yes, perfectly all right. Much better. But for the moment he's mislaid his watch. It'll turn up, of course, but if you'd be good enough to bring one in tomorrow. Any time. No need to wait for visiting hour.'

And now his slippers were removed. Trembling with

weakness, the banker was helped into bed and tucked up like a child, blankets to his chin. He wiped his eyes on the sheet without shame, wondering as he did so, why on earth he had shown such crying need of a watch. On coming here most watches had been removed along with other valuables, for safe keeping. He had hung on to his like grim death, as if he must go on systematically counting every minute and every hour of the twenty-four, for no other reason than that one day this same grim death might wipe them out at one fell swoop when he wasn't looking. On the other hand, he'd lost his watch in the one building where everything went like clockwork: lights-on, bathroom, newspapers, break-fast, washbowls, doctors, therapy, lunch, rest-hour, visitors, doctors, washbowls, supper, visitors, medicine round, bathroom, lights-out.

Now people were beginning to settle themselves for sleep. But the banker was aware of someone on his right. It was the black night nurse who was starting her shift on the two wards, coming round as usual to the beds before lights-out to say goodnight. This flashing, white smile in the dark face bending over him, this intimate, immediate warmth of expression belonged to no part of the world the banker knew, nor did it corre-spond to his experience of his own city or its citizens when they came together for the first time, not knowing one another from Adam. He therefore took the smile thankfully but did not respond wholly in kind. He per-ceived immediately from her expression – both amused and reassuring – that he would not be blamed for this. She understood he wasn't born to it – that was all. He heard a quiet voice: 'Do not distress yourself, Mr Sibald. The watch will arrive in the morning. You will sleep now. Everything will be all right.'

The banker, now flat on his pillow with his eyes tight

shut, was amazed to feel, for the space of a second, one finger moving across his scalp. It was a touch so discreet, so light, it could scarcely be said to fit the word 'stroke'. Then he was alone. He was not a man who pondered much on the meaning or the sound of words. Yet for some time he lay thinking about this word 'stroke'. Over the years the strongest had taken it for themselves, boasting of the club, the sword, the hatchet stroke, the executioner's blade, the missile's deadly curve. Top sportsmen had got hold of the word – rowers and batsmen, champion swimmers and tennis players, all competing for the length, the strength, the rhythm of their stroke. The word belonged to other movements and other states of mind. There was the soft, full stroke of the painter's brush, the quick and fretful stroke of the pen. A stroke was a sudden crisis in the body's blood. It meant falling, stammering and trembling. It was also the touch across the scalp, accompanied by a word or two. It was a single finger smoothing away fear. Now there was silence in the ward. Almost, there was peace. The banker knew that – not excepting the greatest cleric in the land – this was the only touch most of them would wish to feel, the only voice they would choose to hear in the final moments of their life on earth.

The Morning Mare

For some time back the best break in the whole year for Kate had been the short visit to Ireland on her own. No study of the map or talk of any other place could change her mind about this ideal holiday. The town she visited was Dingle in the south-west, where her cousins lived with their parents. It was fun to be with a large family. On her latest stay, however, she found the two oldest boys had just left school and gone to jobs in Dublin. The rest were still at home. Brenda, at sixteen, the oldest girl, was her own age. Two little boys, twin girls in junior school and a ten-month-old baby made up the rest of the family. Kate envied and admired them all. She envied them their black hair, their blue eyes and their casual, colourful clothes. She enjoyed the songs and music of their country, and most of all their stories – admiring the soft or brilliantly cutting edge they could give to the meanest phrase. Mockery and tenderness were here combined, and the sudden, thorny prick of malice. It was useless to try to tell such stories afterwards. They lost their shine and sound, like pebbles carried far inland from a turbulent beach.

The house she visited was an old one, very beautiful, very distinguished – a wreck of a house, needing paint and plaster, needing nails, new pipes, new drains and long, loving care, but getting none. Occasionally someone might make a start on the garden, but after a month or two of rain mixed with the salt wind from the sea, it would become a wilderness again. When the wind was really high a mass of frenzied ivy darkened the graceful frontage of the house and two great twisted thorn bushes would scratch backwards and forwards over the glass of the austere windows. Mosquitoes floated on the sludgy pool where a few perfect water-lilies opened, almost unnoticed, grew brown, and wilted away again. Once, perhaps, the iron gates had creaked open to welcome strangers. In recent years only a few persons had walked, with velvet feet, on paths green with thick moss. Kate liked this place exactly because of the total contrast to her own neat home and its circumspect street with the well-kept gardens. But here, in the land she visited, startling contrasts were near the surface. It was a place of dream and nightmare, cruelty and compassion. Black water could suddenly well up from clear ditches. Huge, ancient rocks jutted from smooth, green fields and blocked the progress of the plough. It was a land where people walked devoutly from church, talking with love and gusto of a pagan past. It was no use trying to have one side without the other. Alternate darkness and light flickered over everything like the weather.

Most of all, even more than the stories and the songs, Kate enjoyed the early morning talks with her cousin Brenda with whom she shared a room. This was the time when the two of them discussed everything – school, work, politics, marriage, careers, happiness, unhappiness, friends, parents and grandparents. Kate's visit coincided with her sixteenth birthday. They woke early that morning and started to talk. They discussed how fifteen might differ from sixteen and even, ridiculously, how sixteen might differ from sixty. They spoke, as usual, about happiness and what exactly it might mean for them. Could they ever get enough of it or would they, sooner or later, fall back into the flat, grey routine where most of their elders seemed to live? 'Some people,' said Brenda, 'think that happiness comes from living absolutely and totally in the present moment – not looking backwards nor forwards.' She insisted it was a business of taking the last drop of sweetness from these moments. On the other hand, happiness might be one instantaneous flash that lit up a whole day, a week, a month or, with luck, even an entire year.

At that instant the milk-van went past the window. It was an old horse-drawn van which Kate, every morning of her visit, had come to dread. She knew by the frenzied clopping of hoofs and the clatter of the milk-cans that it was being driven at the usual breakneck speed up the steep, cobbled street. Always it went so fast that a trickle of milk would escape from the rattling lids while the van would appear to rock precariously from side to side. The horse was a broken-down old nag with a white froth dripping from its lip and a raw patch on one shoulder. Its neighing was like some dreadful high-pitched coughing, most horrible to hear. Kate knew this for a true nightmare and no mistake – an early morning nightmare which would be repeated day after day till the end of her visit. 'I wonder if that horse will drop down dead one of these mornings,' she said over her shoulder to her cousin who was still in bed. 'And I'm not the only one who's seen it,' she added. 'There are people across the way watching from doors and windows. No-one's doing anything. Is *this* the present moment you're wanting me to keep?' At the same time she thought how weak and cowardly it was that she had never run down into the street herself, never called out or gone to the police about the driver and his whip. She had made no move at all. Now she could hardly bear to see her face in the mirror, the pink and white coward that she was!

'Well, never mind,' said Brenda from her bed. 'You can't always choose. Sometimes the present moment isn't good. But look again soon,' she added slyly. 'Maybe it will look better.' Kate couldn't help smiling even while the clattering hoofs still sounded in the distance. The holidays in this part of the world didn't exactly match those back home, and sure enough, two schoolboys from the top class were walking past on their way to a nearby school. Coming from distant farms, they had a long way to go, but every morning they contrived to go more and more slowly as they walked under the window of the girls' bedroom. Sometimes they would walk so slowly they almost stopped. Then together they would look up like two eager, wary young animals, all eyes. They were tall, long-haired youths, sporting sideburns and showing chins and throats that would soon be dark. Their hands were strong and bony with wrists too long for their sleeves. Both appeared to move in awkward mockery of their outgrown gear, at the same time instinctively raising their arms a fraction towards the window in expectation of some future state. For Kate these were the most romantic moments of her visit. She felt the leap of joy as she leaned far out, revealing a soft curve of lace around the sill as the boys stared up. It seemed they stared, steadily, endlessly, totally absorbed and almost vacant-faced in their intentness, as if their cheeks had been wiped blank by a full sponge of milk.

'So you've forgotten about your horse,' said Brenda softly from behind. She was up and standing back in the shadows of the room.

'No, no, I have not!' cried her cousin, 'and if it happens again . . . '

'What then?' asked the other girl.

'I'll do something about it, of course.'

Her cousin said nothing, but smiled to herself as she dressed. It was hot that day. When they went out they found the wet garden steaming. Cascades of drops fell from the bushes as they brushed past. In the morning they roamed about in the woods behind the house, went up the hill with a picnic tea, and in the early evening came down to watch Brenda's father dealing with his swarm of bees which hung from the low branch of a lime tree. Later when it was cooler he gathered the sizzling, brown bundle down into a basket and took them to the hive where he knocked them out cautiously onto the threshold. They knelt down to watch the regiment of bees move slowly up into their furious-sounding retreat. Then they went inside for supper – a rich fish pie with herbs from the garden. Brenda's father was a handsome, heavy, easy-going man who laughed a lot. He talked about the history of the district, he talked about bees, about flowers, sunshine and honey. Late every evening he'd go off to drink, always returning, benign or belligerent by turns.

'What about winter when there's no more honey?' Kate had asked him before he left.

'In the winter I make a special syrup for my bees,' he replied. 'I make great cans of the stuff. It keeps them going till the sun comes out again.'

'Yes, it's the only time he's ever inside the kitchen!' exclaimed Brenda, laughing.

Her mother didn't smile, but with a serious face kept plucking listlessly at the tablecloth. She looked so tired that Kate was only too glad to get up and go off with her cousin again.

'Your mother doesn't listen to your father,' she said when they were outside. 'She doesn't really believe him.'

'No, she doesn't believe him,' Brenda agreed. 'She doesn't believe the honey, sunshine bit. I wouldn't know much about the early time, of course.' Her mother had married later than most, she said. And then she'd worked too hard. One child every twenty months or so had knocked some of the verve and strength from her life.

'I was told everyone helps everyone else here,' said Kate. 'Even the largest families. It goes right down through them all, and the oldest can help the youngest.' All the same, there were days, Brenda had replied calmly, when her mother didn't, simply couldn't get up – not for the life of her. Then, naturally, she herself took over. No, she didn't mind doing dishes, cooking, looking after the others. Not at all. But she didn't think she would ever marry, she added.

'That's rubbish!' said Kate. 'With your looks, your intelligence.'

'Absolutely nothing to do with it,' said her cousin. 'But it's true I've got some talent like my mother.'

She described how her mother had been a true crafts-woman and had brought back some of the old Irish designs into her illuminated scripts and wall-hangings when she started to work on her own. There were tap-estries too, unlike anything that had been seen here before. They had got into exhibitions. One or two had been sent abroad and made a good deal of money. That meant her mother could occasionally go away for longer, visit foreign galleries, sell her work more widely.

'Why doesn't she go on with it then?' asked Kate.

Her cousin laughed at the innocence of this question,

or was it stupidity? Sometimes these were very close to one another, she thought, as she stared at Kate's placid face. 'You don't know much, do you? And you've seen absolutely nothing,' she went on, stretching herself as if the whole subject made her tired and stiff. 'And you're so romantic, it's positively cruel,' she added. Kate couldn't believe that cruelty and romance could ever be spoken about in the same breath. Cruelty was a horse with rolling eyes and froth on its lips. Romance was two boys staring up at a window, and the sound of bees on a summer evening.

'Sleep well then,' were Brenda's last words that night. 'And remember!' Her cousin was almost asleep and so full of the sound of bees, the melting honeycomb and the sun that she couldn't remember what this command might mean.

But in the morning came the cruel awakening. Brenda aroused her cousin with a shout and Kate ran to the window. The coughing, knock-kneed horse went shambling by, the tilting cans clattering. The driver was brandishing his whip. At the back of the room Brenda was sitting bolt upright in bed. 'Do something!' she cried.

'Stop that! Stop!' shouted Kate from the open window. The sunlight was already bright outside. A few shopkeepers were standing at their doors. Otherwise the street seemed unnaturally empty and as sharply focused on man and animal as a snapshot. It was silent too in the country beyond, so silent that every distant sound could be heard – even the early morning train taking people to their work in some far-out district. Kate drew in a deep breath. Oh, to be a brave actor in life rather than an observer! She leant out again. 'Stop!' she shouted down.

The driver looked directly up at the girl. A wide, tilted hat cast a sharp, black angle across his face, but his white teeth flashed a smile. He swept off his hat in a mocking gesture as he galloped past. He cracked the whip again. 'Sorry, sweetheart, but I can't stop today,' he yelled. 'This old mare won't let me!' The stumbling hoofs approached the corner. The frenzied animal went on and disappeared.

Kate sat down on her bed in tears. 'Well, you didn't do much, did you?' said her cousin. 'No use crying about it. Maybe you'll get another chance.' In a few minutes the schoolboys would be coming down the street. Even Brenda felt the anticipation of joy and tried to bring it back for Kate's sake. Now there was a faint whistling and laughter under the window. 'Your friends!' she exclaimed in an encouraging voice. But Kate still sat on the bed, shivering, as if a wintry gust had caught her in midsummer. All sweetness of the momentary romance had suddenly disappeared. Nightmare was galloping through the bright day. Under her window the innocent milk had been spilt around and was trickling slowly through the dust.

This was Kate's last morning before flying home. They spent it happily enough, and in the afternoon her cousin accompanied her to the station where she would catch the train to Dublin.

'Till next autumn then,' said Kate as her train approached. She drew near to kiss her cousin. Brenda seemed to draw back for an instant, cool and unsmiling. 'Next year's visit might have to be postponed,' she said. 'There may be another baby in the family.' Kate was asking questions now, smiling and looking eagerly into her cousin's impassive face. 'I don't want to talk too much about it now,' Brenda explained, 'in case something happens. My mother isn't strong, and she's not so young, you know.' It was obvious Kate didn't know. There was a slight touch of scorn in Brenda's eyes as she said goodbye. Her cousin got up quickly into the train. A gap opened between them now – a gap which was more than the dark, sharp-edged drop between train and platform. For the first time Kate experienced sorrow and fear of this wounding gash. On the platform Brenda was standing very straight and still. She looked suddenly thinner, harder and older as if she came from a country more mysterious, unexplored, and much more complex than her cousin had ever imagined. When the train started to move Kate leaned out and waved with a gentle, reassuring gesture. But Brenda held her arm straight up without waving. Indeed it seemed a salute rather than a wave and before the train left the station she had turned swiftly on her heel and disappeared.

Connections

9 *I* have always been an extremely cautious man – physically, mentally, emotionally. Surely I don't have to describe this state of things. Still, I *will* explain for the benefit of those who won't admit to sharing my particular traits. My work as a dentist is exacting. My mind must be totally concentrated on one small part of my patient's anatomy, and being sociable is not my particular line. I don't like unexpected emotion to catch me out either. I have to have steady hands. I don't even care to think about something that might keep me awake past my usual time for sleep. I *do* sleep, I may say, whenever I get the chance. But I don't dream and I'm not interested in other people's dreams, neither the daytime nor the night-time ones. Yes, as I sat in the station waiting for the connection back to the city, I fell asleep for a few seconds. It can hardly be called a proper station of course. There are two narrow, windswept platforms and one bleak waiting room. People cross to it over a muddy bit of field from a little-used bus route. And the buses have this unusual property of seldom, if ever, connecting with the trains.

An over-fanciful friend of mine told me that when he sits in this God-forgotten station he thinks of all the lost connections throughout his life – those important business transactions cut off while still hardly begun, the hoped-for connection in friendship or in love never achieved, some family tie, dropped for half a lifetime, more irretrievable as the years go by. Personally, I can't afford to think of such things, and I've heard all the absurd stories about the suicidal depression of dentists who feel loved by no-one. The truth is that any dentist who relieves an aching tooth is likely to be loved with an intensity that few romantic poets could possibly express in the whole course of their writing lives. Well, I myself am not into the imagination bit. It is not necessarily a help in my work. Furthermore, I have been told by people who know, that this imagination, and all the things that go with it, can be a most diabolically debilitating thing. Indeed, those who fall for it assure me that, in time, this faculty can actually make the knees very feeble and the legs perfectly useless. I stand most of the day and my legs are important to me. I know there are lines somewhere about supporting the feeble knee, but obviously there is no way I could do this for myself in the middle of work, and my young receptionist – rather a modest girl – would certainly be embarrassed if asked to do it for me.

Long after the particular incident I will be speaking of, my friend told me that an old man had opened a coffee stall on this forbidding platform. If so, I suppose he must have been some sort of saint, for there was no money in it. All that was said about him was that his coffee was boiling hot and that he had a kind face. If you let on you were brokenhearted you could get a sausage roll on the side, and at a very reasonable price. If disaster had struck he laid on the chutney free. He was no fool, of course. He soon noticed everyone wanted chutney whether their disaster was huge or minuscule.

Well, after a few seconds on the station bench I woke with strange words in my ear – six words, lightly spoken, but all perfectly clear: 'I think I broke my heart'

– as if dropped from the tail-end of a dream. They were certainly not my words, being totally out of character – not the way I'd express myself even in a dream. I turned up my collar briskly, took a look at my watch and found there was another fifteen minutes to go before the train. Then I looked at the iron bridge over the track and saw another passenger labouring across. He was making very heavy weather of it, I must say, struggling with his great, clumsy suitcase – sometimes heaving it forward with his knee and now and then putting it down to get his breath before he reached the end of the bridge. Even at that distance I could hear him groaning and panting in rather an ominous way. I myself gave a groan, but it was the groan of an incurably cautious man. For that's always the way of it. Persons like myself, who hope never to get mixed up in anything outside our own concerns, can be presented, out of the blue, with a problem. We know we are expected to rise at once to our feet and help other people over bridges and across roads, help them hump their huge bags, bundles and cases, get them into cars, trains and buses, lift them on to bicycles, assure them, assist them, and hold them up in every possible way. It's the lame-dogs-over-stiles threat that our kind must watch out for. While others are running, caring and helping, we are usually sitting down doing absolutely damn all – and what's more – hoping against hope to keep it that way. Nevertheless I did get to my feet – I'll say that for myself. I strolled towards the bridge. 'No hurry!' I called cheerfully. 'Train's not due for another ten minutes!' Though I made no effort to meet him he seemed reassured. He slowed down. His breathing grew lighter. At last he came off the bridge and moved towards the bench where he sat down.

'What place is this?' he enquired calmly. I didn't

answer, not because I was determined not to talk, but because opposite us on the other side was a great board with the name of the station – huge, black letters on white. I myself, at this distance in time, don't remember the place and never wish to remember it.

We sat for some time in silence with his great, clumsy case between us. My dear aunt had always maintained I am an awkward person – a mass of contradictions. For instance, I don't like endless talk and I don't like long silences either. Both can be fearfully disturbing. Perhaps this man was one of those who found silence more disturbing than talk. At any rate he began to speak with some effort: 'Do you know these parts?'

'Not well,' I replied. 'I've just been visiting.'

'Relations or just friends?' he asked.

I gave a laugh. It struck me as a strange way to put it. '*Just* friends,' I repeated. 'You mean you think relatives are always better than friends?'

'I wouldn't know,' he said. 'I've neither the one nor the other.'

'Of course, relations can sometimes be more difficult than friends,' I said. But I didn't care to take the argument further. I liked my one eccentric aunt and had no intention of discussing her with a stranger. 'So where do *you* come from?' I asked.

'Never from any distance,' he replied, 'on account of the weight of this case. I can't move with it. Can't go running around like some people.'

He knew nothing about me, of course, yet I sensed a reproof in that 'running around', as if a middle-aged dental practitioner can live a gay, carefree life! Certainly at my stage I have a little more leisure. But nowadays I can help to bring beginners on. I demonstrate how old methods can reinforce the new. I didn't tell him what I did, of course. I've heard all those bad old jokes about dentists more times than I've pulled bad old teeth. So I said nothing. Anyway, I suppose I am not good company, being accustomed to my silent patients who, on command, open their mouths as wide as they possibly can – but are never allowed to speak a word.

'I think I'll take a stroll up the platform. It's very cold down here,' I said. Indeed, old tickets were scuttling around the place like leaves, and ancient posters, advertising glorious summer tours with golden women, were tearing strips off glamour and flapping furiously from the walls.

'Then I'll not come with you,' my companion replied. 'As I told you, I can hardly move with this, and we're not supposed to leave our cases around.'

I went off, looking back once. He sat, fingers spread on his knees, his jaw jutting out like an awkward patient in the dental chair. Perhaps he was listening for the train or just to my retreating footsteps. As a matter of fact I wouldn't have minded having a third person around. I looked across the bridge to the twinkling lights of a distant town, but I knew there would be nobody else that evening.

I had to keep looking back at him, I don't know why. I didn't know the man, didn't particularly like him, in fact. But somehow I wanted his company. At that moment, as I walked the grey platform, I experienced a fearful pang of loneliness. Needing the man's company, yet walking away because I didn't wish to admit it. Wanting the silence yet dreading it at the same time. He had brought out all the contradictions in me – this man with his heavy case and his light voice. Yes, I wanted his company. Desperately. Or as the desperate need the despairing. 'If I hadn't such a heavy load I could escape as quickly as you did,' he remarked with a slightly mocking smile as I came back. I wondered for a moment if he were on the run. He had the sunless pallor of a convict.

'You sound like a wanted man,' I remarked with an attempt at flippancy.

'Heavens, no, I'm not wanted! Who would want *me*?' He gave me a sharp look. 'Except yourself, perhaps,' he added, 'because you're frightened of something. You want company on this platform, don't you? Why? Yes, yes, it's because you're frightened of something. Because you're frightened of *me* perhaps. Well now, that's a strange state of affairs! Doesn't make sense at all, does it? I expect you want everything to make sense, to have some kind of co-ordination in your life. But one day you'll have to meet something that doesn't add up, that doesn't fit in, that has no connection at all with anything else. Like that dreary waiting room out there – truly, *une salle des pas perdus*.'

So he was going to start airing his French at this hour, in this place, I said to myself. That would be the last straw. But he was silent again, staring gloomily at his feet. 'Let's both go to the end of the platform and back,' I suggested. 'It's not only company I'm talking about. It's the exercise. Anyway, I think you've got me wrong. Certainly I like order and efficiency. How otherwise would I get on? And I like to see the way ahead.'

He shrugged his thin shoulders and looked towards the fields where a mist was creeping in from the sea. 'Do you see far ahead at this moment?' he asked. 'No, I'm not going to leave my case, and I can't move one more step.' He gave a slight smile. 'I am a china man,' he murmured. 'By that I mean that I carry several kinds of china from branch to branch of my firm – saucers and cups, plates and sometimes even teapots. Oh, nothing delicate, of course. Just thick, damnably heavy, hideously ugly stuff. I don't imagine you'd like it.'

'Well, never mind,' I said. 'At least I can help you for a yard or two.' As I put my fingers round the handle he gave a strange, withdrawing gasp. As for me, I braced myself, clenched the muscles of my arm and lifted the case up. It came off the ground like a winged thing. 'Why, it's as light as air!' I cried. 'Too heavy to carry indeed! There's nothing inside, is there?'

He lifted his head, smiling, in the yellow light. Indeed he looked both black and yellow – black hollows for the eyes and mouth, his teeth a shining yellow with black gaps. It is part of my profession to notice such things. Even his smile reminded me of those rather ghastly and unnatural smiles an excessively polite patient will give a dentist after having endured a good deal in the reclining chair.

'Oh yes,' he said. 'Light enough *now*, perhaps. But when I was alive it was *immensely* heavy. I think it broke my heart,' he added like the casual afterthought of everything he'd said before.

Naturally, I didn't let on I'd heard the things he'd just uttered, didn't let on I'd heard a single word, in fact. They made absolutely no sense, you see – had no con-nection with anything else at all. Thank goodness, how-ever, there are ways of dealing with nonsense. The best way is to ignore it and say nothing. So now there was complete silence between us – so deep a silence that very far off I heard the train like muffled thunder from the distant hills.

'You will help me on when it comes, of course,' he said, turning his head to the sound. My heart was beat-ing fast, but I spoke in my usual decisive voice. I was not unkind. For was his case not featherlight?

'I help *nobody*,' I said.

'Ah then – no need to worry yourself,' he softly replied. 'There is *nobody* here.'

Where Is the Sun?

ow did Mr Paul Renwick – a young account-ant, seemingly full of commonsense and with a sound enough grasp of History, Physics, Mathematics, as well as a smattering of Astronomy – how did he come to imagine that the sun might disappear from the sky between one day and the next? There had been much nuclear talk in the last months, of course, talk of a darkness over the earth, of a slow but steady shadowing of sun, moon and stars in a still dateless future. Certainly he'd been in a strange bedroom on a little-known coastal area of south-west Scotland. But that didn't mean that the entire visible universe could turn upside down. It was true that he'd not long recovered from a crisis of nerves – not a devastating one, but enough to reduce the normality of everyday things. On this short winter holiday he'd woken suddenly in the night, got up and drawn aside the curtain. Naturally he saw exactly what he expected to see following a fine sunny day. He was looking into a perfectly cloudless sky and at a full moon white as a polished plate against a clear space full of brilliant stars. In these dark spaces he could make out a few familiar planets and constellations. He saw more clearly than ever before the belt of Orion and its blurred nebula beneath. Away to the east he picked out sharply the seven visible stars of the Pleiades. This was the moment he got it firmly into his head that the morning would be as clear as the night, the coming day as dazzling as the previous one.

Not that he always expected to see the sun in this country. No, he was used to dark midwinter breaks and even to sunless summer holidays. But it had been a mistake to get up suddenly in the midst of a deep sleep to look out. He had gone back immediately to bed and to God knows what strange nightmares.

When he woke up that morning he was astonished to view an ominous purple-black sea spreading slowly over an ashen beach. The sky was thunderously dark. The expected sun was not there – only an eerie shaft of white light slanting between black clouds and illuminating what appeared to be a vast hole in mid-ocean. Once, a permanent and fatal darkness had been forecast for the earth, and this was surely it. Renwick now moved rapidly about the strange bedroom with wildly beating heart, trying to find slippers and dressing-gown. He opened his bedroom door and stepped out into the corridor. There were a few early risers around, some getting ready for an early stroll before breakfast. 'Oh my God!' cried Renwick to the first person he set eyes on, 'where is the sun?' This man – a retired headmaster from the city – had heard many complaints about the weather in his time, but never from a pale-faced, bare-footed stranger before breakfast. He noted with astonishment that the young man was still in blue-striped pyjamas, that his eyes were wild, and that his uncombed hair seemed spiked with a peculiar panic. Silently he dropped his eyes to the twisted white feet on the crimson carpet. By this time the headmaster's wife had emerged from the bedroom behind.

The young man, as if appealing to a softer spirit, directed his terrible cry and his fierce gaze towards her. 'There is no sun!' He stood watching her, hoping for the comfort of a similar terror in another human face. But, though female, she was not a softer spirit. She inclined her head in his direction for a moment, smiled distantly, and remarked, 'It seems a little cloudy this morning and I believe it might rain before noon. I hope we didn't make an unfortunate choice this year. Majorca fell through at the last minute, you see. That's the only reason we're here, of course, and we'll just have to make the best of it, I suppose.'

The idea of Majorca having fallen through appeared to terrify the young man more than ever. He ran down the steep flight of stairs to the landing below shouting, 'There is no sun today! The sun has gone!' One formidable waiter who was coming up, brutally intent on breaching the DO NOT DISTURB doors on the floor above, looked him up and down with disapproval. 'May I get you a dressing gown, sir, and your slippers?' Paul Renwick went down a further flight to a landing overlooking the ground floor where many fully-dressed persons were drifting their way to the dining room, slowly, dreamily, and almost bouncily – the way hungry people might walk steered by an empty stomach, as by a balloon. The waiter, following the young man, put his tray on the landing table, flew down into the hall where he removed his own waterproof from a cupboard and came back with it over his arm. This he flung with resentful generosity over the shoulders of Renwick as he stumbled towards the breakfast room.

The large room was already half full. Because of the undoubted darkness of the morning, the lights were on. But these were not people easily disturbed, not people to show emotion of any kind at this time of day. In other words, these were northerners. Certain adjectives had been applied to them, and they were proud of it. They had been called dour, undemonstrative, canny, common-sensible, moral, reliable, God-fearing, businesslike and unimpeachably white. Just now they were hidden behind morning newspapers which emphasised these qualities in their pages. Who would have imagined that in the midst of such reading they would have been forced into the embarrassment of hearing a hoarse voice shout from the doorway, 'The sun is gone! It will not be coming up again!' To make matters worse, this man, standing in a shabby outsize waterproof, was accompanied by the head waitress who had found a prominent seat for him, and by a waiter who was trying to fix a pair of very small slippers onto his bare feet.

Now the waiter gave up. A woman in overalls – her cheeks hot from the kitchen stove – had been summoned to bring other slippers and to perform this intimate task. A woman kneeling at the feet of a man was fine in a shoe shop. Between strangers an exchange about the weather, even about a missing sun, might pass. Anything more was unnecessary. The fact that the slippers belonged to the woman, that they were very loose with fluffy red pompoms, gave many an uneasy sensation. Quickly they shifted their eyes to the papers again.

The main article seemed an unnecessarily unpleasant one that morning. The gist of it was that every living creature on the earth would one day disappear following some catastrophic, man-made happening. The seas would boil, the rocks vaporise, the cities be reduced to cinders. All green grass and leaf would be stripped in a flash. Ferocious winds would scour the planet. For those with still unmelted eyes to search for them – moon, stars and sun would be obscured for centuries on end. Darkness would reign on earth. Darkness and utter silence.

One breakfaster, already irritated that his kipper was

burnt to a frazzle on one side and his toast barred with black, stared at the newcomer over his paper and remarked to his wife that it was high time a doctor was called to the scene. But this was about to happen. The young man in loose red slippers, who had been given a seat near the door, looked up to see a waiter hurrying over with another coffee. He was followed in a few minutes by a distinguished-looking elderly man who was invited to sit down at Renwick's table. Obviously he had been invited to reassure the late guest. There was a certain authority about the older man. He might have been a doctor, a clergyman, a psychiatrist, a headmaster or even a judge – a man obviously used to dealing with awkward persons. Another coffee was poured for him and he leaned confidently across the table. 'I believe you have a problem – no doubt a very disturbing one as we all have sometime or other. You wonder whether you will ever see the sun again. Is that it? It is probably not as uncommon as you imagine. Perhaps, as a child, you were terrified by some fantastic story. Maybe you were once shut up by yourself in the dark – punished, no doubt, for something you never did. I think that may well be part of your problem.'

'No, perhaps it's God's problem,' said Renwick. 'Perhaps the whole cosmic mechanism is all jammed up. I hope it's nothing to do with us. I hope we haven't messed things up ireparably.' When his counsellor heard this last word and had assured himself that his companion knew something of the meaning of it, his face lost something of its paternal expression. 'Still,' murmured the young man, 'they're probably working like mad to get it started up again.'

His would-be adviser looked uneasy about the word 'they'. He had no idea what might be meant by it – whether angels or devils or some anonymous company of heavenly but irate engineers. He tried a more practical approach.

'You do realise, don't you, that the midwinter sun is totally different from the midsummer one. Anyway, I'll grant you the day is very overcast. It's as simple as that. Have another coffee with me. Before long everything will look normal again.' Renwick stared around him at the dark windows, the electric lights overhead, the grimly frowning faces hiding behind black headlines. He knew that, for him, nothing would ever look simple again, far less, normal.

'How about taking a step outside with me after you've drunk your coffee?' suggested the other. 'You'll see what I mean by midwinter darkness. I can lend you a warm gaberdine,' he went on, 'and a pair of my old galoshes in the hall, big enough to go over those slippers.' His young table companion finished his coffee quietly and together they left the dining room. For a split second every newspaper in the place shifted sideways with a huge sighing sound like the stealthy lift of dozens of grey wings. A visible relief flew over the place. Meanwhile the young man waited in the hall while his companion disappeared into the hall cupboard and came out again with a pair of large galoshes and a gaberdine.

'I can't quite work out exactly what's wrong with him,' one guest who was near the open dining-room door remarked to her husband, 'but I can see it has something to do with shoes. They've done nothing but put different ones on and off him ever since he came downstairs.'

'Probably simply forgot to pack any,' said her husband going back to his paper. 'There's nothing gives you such a shocking turn as coming away to the wilds, miles and miles from home, and not a single thing to put on your feet. I lost my own shoes once for only half a day but I honestly felt the solid earth had totally disappeared. Simply didn't have a clue how to put one foot in front of the other!'

The man in the hall and his older companion now seemed to be moving away. For a moment they paused in the doorway, looking out. 'That's right,' said the porter who'd heard a garbled tale of darkness and panic. 'A breath of fresh air will do you a world of good.' When the two had left he gave his own theory to his mate at the opposite side of the door.

'Could be sudden blindness,' he said. 'I heard of a man not so long ago – woke up in the morning and couldn't see one bloody thing in front of him. Couldn't find his money, couldn't find his specs. Gone blind in the night, you see. Oh yes, it can happen. *Anything* can happen!'

'At any time, and to anyone!' his opposite number finished with some relish.

But outside the young man Renwick was staring at the sky with open eyes. 'You see,' said his comforter. 'It's simply a dark, midwinter morning, as I told you. The sun's a long, long time coming out – that's all. In fact the total absence of the sun is an absolute impossibility. It has never happened since life began. Why should it happen now?'

In his borrowed, black galoshes the young man began to jump on the dark sand and wave his arms about. 'Because *now* we're geniuses and madmen, of course. No dawdling, no pondering. Chaos can come in a single flash. Oceans will be pulled to the tops of mountains, the shells and rocks ground to a red-hot powder. What does that remind you of? Does it remind you of Hell?'

'I have never been in Hell,' said the other, keeping his voice as cool and placating as a Sunday school teacher.

'The brains in the baby's skull will sizzle, the marrow dry up in the young man's bones,' Renwick went on. 'Some of these have *already* happened. Did you say "Why should it happen *now*?".'

He gave the older man a warning push. At this the other stopped in his tracks. 'Don't push me too far. I'm trying to be patient, to be helpful. Do you think I want to be out here with you in the middle of my holiday? The fact is I really don't care for folk who must dramatise themselves and everything else. Losing a pair of slippers is one thing. Thinking the skies will fall and the seas dry up because you can't lay your hands on them is another. I'm not a genius – simply a good teacher and I'm not ashamed to say it, though I know you've a thing against cleverness. I'm going in now. I need my holiday like everyone else. Thanks to you I haven't even had a decent breakfast yet.'

True, behind them the hotel, still blazing with lights, looked inviting. Breakfast smells and the clatter of knives and forks still reached them from the open door. The young man was quiet now, staring away from the open sea. Far up on the beach, yesterday's sand castles were still intact. Even the high Babel tower, decorated with white and green stones and tipped with a gull's feather, had stood firm during the night. Some of the highest footsteps had been preserved. So had the smiling, fat sand-faces with their shell-bright eyes and seaweed hair.

Now the older man gripped his companion's elbow cautiously and, gingerly pinching the sleeve of his coat between finger and thumb, turned him around and steered him back towards the building behind.

'Are you walking better then?' said the porter at the door. 'The feet can be an awful trial on holiday – that's for sure.' Once inside, Renwick flung off the newly acquired gaberdine while his companion retired to the dining room for another coffee. On the first landing Renwick removed the galoshes and dropped the pom-pommed slippers softly over the bannister. On the second landing he discarded both waterproof and gaberdine. To his surprise he felt both lightened and warm as if these things had not clothed him, but instead hidden him from some benign influence in the upper atmosphere. Now he climbed easily forward, like an out-of-depth swimmer forced to discard his restricting clothes to save his life – then finding suddenly that he is not dying of cold at all but is actually warmer in the deep sea. Slowly he went on up to the dark landing with its closed doors and found that his own familiar slippers had been laid neatly outside his own room. He put them on quickly then paused, unbelieving, as he glimpsed the shining line of bright orange beneath the door. This he opened and stepped through a shaft of brilliant sunlight. A young woman was pulling aside the curtain and, low down on the horizon, a huge, red sun was breaking through black clouds. On either side of her – sitting on the wide sill, heads pressed to the window pane – was a small girl and boy. All three turned round to him, smiling like angels in an Italian painting suddenly disturbed in the business of Annunciation. While the brightness grew the mother's arm was still raised to lift the curtain, letting the sleeve of her loose, blue blouse fall to her elbow. It was the light, familiar gesture belonging to his childhood, but now seeming extraordinarily powerful – revealing the unfamiliar and unpredictable day ahead.

Paul Renwick went further into his room without even answering a pleasantry about the weather, and sat down silently on his bed.

'I'm feeling faint,' he said. Immediately the tableau in

the window changed. The woman dropped the curtain, and, at a sign, the children slid to the ground.

'Lie right down,' she said. 'Don't mind us.' Obediently, Renwick lay back on top of his bed. Again, he had his shoes removed.

'What an odd thing!' he exclaimed. 'Do you know that ever since I got up people have done nothing but take off and put on various kinds of shoe for me – some soft, some hard, but none of them fitting.'

'Well, that's the trouble,' she said. 'I dare say you should never have got up this morning. You should simply have rung this bell and let them bring breakfast to your room. By the way, have you *had* anything at all to eat?'

'One cup of coffee,' he replied opening his eyes, 'and afterwards a walk on the beach.'

'It could be the reason for feeling faint,' she said. 'First getting up too quickly, too early. Then nothing to eat on top of it.' The children were now peering at him over her shoulder as at a waxen exhibit in a glass case.

'Look, I'm going to get you something decent to eat,' she said. 'I'll be back in a moment. If you feel worse just touch the bell.' She hustled the children out before her and the young man lay still, watching the shaft of sunlight moving across the floor towards his bed. Fifteen minutes later the woman returned carrying a teapot, cup and saucer, toast, butter and marmalade on a tray.

'I don't think I can take it unless you have some yourself,' said Renwick.

'Don't bother,' the girl replied. 'We have ours later when all the breakfasts are finished. But, if it worries you, of course I will. There's only one cup though.' She fetched the glass from the basin shelf, pulled up a chair and sat down. As she poured tea she told the story of herself, as a young wife, pouring boiling, new-made jam into a glass jar – and, seconds after, the crack like a pistol shot. The next-door neighbour had come in suddenly just seconds after. 'Well, she would, wouldn't she?' the girl remarked. 'Just as I was wiping the stuff off the kitchen table and picking bits of glass from a boiling mess of strawberries.'

'I hope this is all right,' said Renwick, thinking of the intruding neighbour's sudden appearance. 'I mean the two of us sitting together in my bedroom. Total strangers and all that.'

'Don't worry,' said the woman. 'In our work we know everything that can possibly happen between two persons in one bedroom – natural, unnatural and super-natural. We've had the lot, in fact. We've had the steal-ing, the stabbing and the rape, birth, death, fear, fighting and just plain madness. But, when a man and a woman can't have a cup of tea together, I'd say the whole thing's finished – civilisation packed up. Bomb or no bomb, it's the crash, the split, the final crack-up!'

'Do you think so?' Renwick replied mildly, helping himself to another slice of toast. Now he told her the strange story of the sun's disappearance, of the daz-zlingly clear night followed by the black morning. The woman showed no surprise. She listened to his tale of the sunless world, the great galoshes and the ill-fitting coat that was not his own. She remained calm and sad.

'You have felt all this darkness yourself?' he asked.

'How can you ask? I have two small children. In five months there will be another. Of course I've felt and feared that particular darkness every single day.'

Meanwhile the sun had spread across the wall, the red carpet, the white bed and pillows, while making every separate item on the tray shine with its own light – the white cup scooped out of deep blue shadow, the bowl of sugar with its silver spoon, the burnished, gold-flecked jar of thick-cut marmalade. The man and woman stared at each object as if seeing it for the first time or the last. Light struck a corner of the mirror and the woman got up and walked across. 'I'll have to go now,' she said, pinning some loose strands into the nape of her neck. 'My husband goes to the building site in twenty minutes.'

'What sort of building is he on?' asked Renwick.

'New houses at the moment. But sometimes, of course, schools, hospitals, churches – whatever comes up.'

'I'm not too interested in churches myself,' said Renwick. 'There's hardly a cleric in the land who's got a word to say about the earth's end. And I'm not speaking about the old hellfire ranters. So they're still building churches, are they? Even if every one of them vanishes in a wind of fire?'

She put a hand up to her face as if half-ashamed of herself. 'I know we should all be out with banners. We should be writing letters and getting up on platforms. And yet – it may seem strange to you – not being a married man – but there's an amazing lot to do between getting the children to school and bringing them back. The hotel job is nothing – only an hour or two. The lunch pack for my husband is made early. After the kids go off there's the beds to make, the cleaning, the washing, doing out the fire and laying it. There's the shopping, of course, before I get the children back. There's always something going round the school of course – more than just colds, I mean. There are the usual infections and things more serious than that. One or two neighbours might look in for a chat during the afternoon. I like that, of course. It all sounds nothing at all, and there's no way I can make it sound earth-shaking. I can only say it goes on, day in, day out. Most people, helping here part-time, have exactly the same sort of life. It's very tiring and there's no way women can ever explain what's so important about it. When I took this job it seemed like a wonderful change. At first it felt like freedom, but I'd clean forgotten I had to fit in all the other things as well.'

Suddenly the sun shone full on a side-mirror and for a moment they were blinded. The woman turned from the mirror with a wide smile, her face glowing in the outside sun and from the reflected sun within. 'So you see we've got two suns now. We are all safe.' She went out, carefully shutting the door behind her.

Now, alone in his room, the young man remembered a third sun – the heroic human face, the most easily extinguished, the first to go out in darkness. 'Just press the bell,' the girl had said. Yet if the entire earth should put its finger on a panic bell? What good would that do? There would be such a clangour of fury and fear, such warnings, church bell peals, such cries for mercy, such carrying away of children and babies. And all to no purpose.

Now there was little noise in the hotel. Late break-fasters were coming back upstairs, chatting for a while on each landing before they closed their doors. Behind some doors arguments broke out as to how the day should be spent. Then there was silence again.

Suddenly there was a light tap on Renwick's door. He got up to find a small boy standing outside with a newspaper in his hand. 'My mum says you'll not have seen the paper today. They've read it. She says to keep it.' Having given his message and handed over the paper, he turned and ran downstairs – looking back once to stare steadily at Renwick's face, then at his pyjamas and at the frayed hole in one knee. Then he ran on, ready for school and smugly tidy himself.

Paul Renwick examined the paper. It had black headlines all right, but few hints of horrors. Only far-off scandals were cited. Praise for its own country was discreet but clear and it was taken as read that it was superior to its neighbour across the border. Renwick had heard it all before. He had lived for years in Northern Ireland long before the recent troubles began. He had read the papers and listened to his friends there. The gist of it was that across the border in the south of Ireland he would notice it was different not only politically, but in every human way. It was true, they admitted, they themselves might not have the same gifts as the people of the south who had charm for instance, and the capacity to act, sing and talk with wit and poetry. But what was charm compared to their own honesty? Renwick had no doubt these comparisons went on across borders in every part of the world. Different virtues would be compared and different vices.

He went back to the paper in his hand. It was not exactly a rag. There were no pin-ups, no religious or racial prejudice. There was a kind of mild, comfortable reality about it. Here were the familiar domestic illnesses and how to deal with them, how to look after pets, how to cater for parties and awkward family gatherings. There were snippets about entertainment for children. There was a long, solemn article about Keeping the Peace. This had nothing to do with wars. It was about keeping the peace between husbands and wives, fathers and sons, mothers and daughters, brothers and sisters and even between life-long friends. There were special sections about Housework, Homework, Job Hunting, Decorating. Renwick flicked through the pages quickly. It was dull, the language trite, the sentiments and solutions absolutely predictable. Certain pages were disparaging towards women, while the romantic streak curled through them like soft, pink ribbon. Once in a while the moral note was struck with a resounding clang that echoed down through columns of short and pithy bite-sized sermons for each hour of the day. Renwick had long suspected there were two kinds of madness – the mad belief in all the horrors that might happen to the earth itself, and the mad complacency that this could never happen. The paper he held in his hand came somewhere between the two outlooks. It dealt with day-to-day trials and tried to find a simple cure.

And it had other uses. At the end of every calm or turbulent day it could be twisted up neatly, economically, and used for kindling tomorrow's fire.

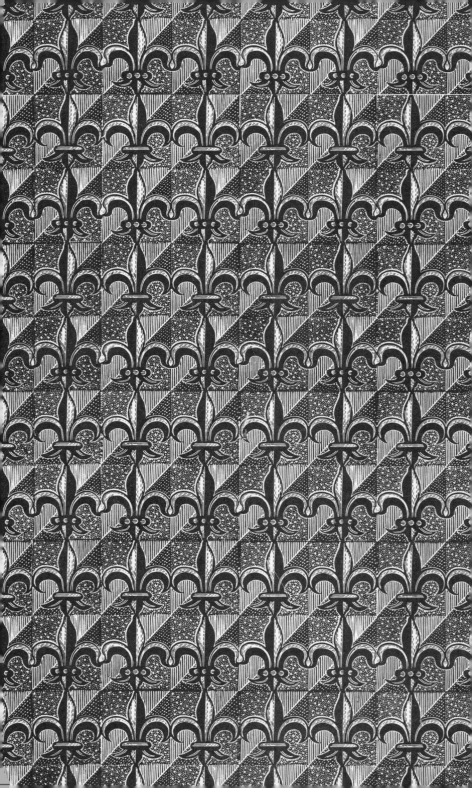